CORMAC

HARRISON AMBUSH BOOK 2

KATHI S. BARTON

This is a work of fiction. Names, characters, places, and incidents are products of the author's imagination or are used fictitiously and are not to be construed as real. Any resemblance to actual events, locations, organizations, or persons, living or dead, is entirely coincidental.

World Castle Publishing, LLC
Pensacola, Florida
Copyright © Kathi S. Barton 2016
Hardback ISBN: 9781629893761
Paperback ISBN: 9781629893778
eBook ISBN: 9781629893785
First Edition World Castle Publishing, LLC, February 8, 2016
http://www.worldcastlepublishing.com
Cover: Karen Fuller
Editor: Eric Johnston
Editor: Maxine Bringenberg

CHAPTER 1

"It says right here that this is the way we are supposed to do it. Not the way you're showing us. I need for you to back away from the equipment and let me do it my way. That's what is going to work," Elton grumbled. Mac wondered if he found Stormy and asked her to shoot this man, if she would do it. *Of course she would*, he thought. *And would smile while doing it.* "You can't tell me that your way is better when I know better. You're just trying to mess things up for me."

"Oh, but I can and I am. There is nothing saying that we can't improve on the way this line is run. And this way, the way that you've been doing it up until now, is why this business is losing money. And losing money is the best way for them to close down and for you to be out of a job." The man only huffed at him, pointing out yet again that the instructions said that his way was the most efficient way. "Yes, it might have been, fourteen years ago when you had this equipment put in. But short of putting in an entire new work line, you're going to have to trust me on this. I know better."

"So you say, but I'm under the opinion that you don't know what you're talking about. I don't know why you were hired in the first place. You know nothing about this production line, and as soon as I can convince my bosses — and I will — that you have this all screwed up, we're going to go back to doing it the correct way anyway." Mac stood up straighter and felt his cat run along his skin. "You can get huffy with me all you want, but I know what is best for this company. I've been working here since their father opened the doors, and I'll be working here long after they're bored with it and go about their business."

Mac said nothing, but moved away from the man as he pulled out his phone. He had to talk to someone who was reasonable, and dialed the first number on his phone. When Storm answered, he had to smile. From the sound of her voice, she wasn't having any better of a time than he was.

"Did you know that when you put a box on the line that there are all kinds of infrared lights that can read not only what's in the box, but even where the fuck it's supposed to be going? That the system is specifically made to do just that?" He told her he did, as a matter of fact. "Well, smart ass, did you know why it's not working here at Ship It? The reason why we were called in to fix it?"

"The machines aren't calibrated? The lights are too bright around it to let it be read properly? There are any number of reasons for it not to work." She snorted at him, something that he'd come to love about her. It conveyed so much, her snort. "Why is it not working at Ship It?"

"They turned it off. I mean, like they just went to the line, tore out all the wiring, and then turned it off at the computer system when it kept telling them that it didn't work. Not only that it wasn't working, but also exactly where it wasn't working. And now you have to ask me why they would turn off a multimillion dollar piece of very important equipment when they advertise that that's what they use to get your packages to you on time?" He started to laugh, telling her he had no idea. "It didn't match their uniform shirts that they're required to wear when they work. The red—and this is no fucking lie—the red clashed so badly with the orange shirts that the owner's daughter complained. Because she picked the color and hated the way it looked when the boxes went by. How fucking stupid do you have to be? I'm not kidding you. It's a good thing you made me leave my gun at my house when you sent me here. Otherwise, we'd be calling in the big time lawyers that I'd need for a lawsuit. Someone would have been dead about ten minutes ago. What's up with you? Did you tell them what they have to do to improve their work situation?"

"Pretty much the same thing you're running into there. This guy in charge while the family is still learning the ropes said that his way is right because that's the way they've been doing it for years. I'm pretty sure that this guy doesn't even own a computer or a smart phone. It wasn't the way he was raised or some shit." Mac moved to his temporary office at the plant and began gathering his things. Time to meet up with the family soon, and he had to get back home anyway. "I'm going to take the next flight out after I get finished with the family. If they want us to come here again, it's going to be when that guy is gone. Or they're fucked."

"Good luck. And don't forget about tomorrow. I have that meeting with my attorneys and you have to sign the paperwork on the building we're buying there." He nodded, then told her he'd be there. "Also, my friend is going to start working tomorrow, too, full-time. If you have a minute, go by the Home Cooking and see if she's settling in all right for me. Riordan and I won't be home until day after tomorrow, as we have to swing by the White House for a minute."

He thought of that. Swing by the White House like it was right on the way home from the grocery. Stormy would even be able to go on up to the family residence once she was there, and hell, more than likely she and Riordan would be having dinner there with the president, and maybe even a drink or two.

"I'll take care of it for you on this end. Where am I meeting the attorneys for the building? And I can't tell you again how much I hate that you've done this. I could have just gotten a loan for it on my own. You didn't have to buy it for the shop I have in mind." She snorted again and he smiled. "I wonder if when you have children that'll be their answer to everything you ask them, too."

"More than likely. But since your mom and dad are telling me now that they're going to be baby-sitting every chance they get, I'm pretty sure that your mom will get them out of the habit. But that doesn't mean I'm going to not tell them to do it around her as much as they can. You know, just for fun." Mac didn't doubt that for a single minute.

Mac had to meet with the new owners of one of the oldest toy firms in the downtown area of Atlanta. They'd been shipping out retro toys for the last several decades, getting them cheaply and helping fill a lot of stores opening up with their new line. But they were behind in their shipment dates, so much so that they'd called him to see what was wrong with their line. It only took him ten minutes of working the line to know what the problem was. But Mac had worked for the two weeks he said he would. The bottle neck in the entire operations was due to one man.

He was shown to the office of Bryon and Noreen Stokes as soon as he entered the building.

"We were hoping to see you before you left. I understand that you've been working on getting our lines right. I hope it wasn't too much trouble for you." Bryon smiled at him. "Elton Coltrane called a few minutes ago. He said that you'd left there in a huff and that he didn't think you'd figured out anything. I'm pretty sure that you'd be a little more professional than just leaving when you couldn't find what was wrong. I'm sure you tried."

"Is that what Elton told you? That I didn't find anything wrong?" Bryon looked at his sister and then back at him, nodding. "I see. Well, I am a professional, as you said, but if you have some time, I'd like to go over my findings with you."

"Of course."

Mac was led to a large conference room with a table big enough for his family to have dinner at. Noreen was the younger of the two siblings, but Mac knew that she was the one with the business sense while her brother was the one with the big ideas. Which blended well with the two of them. She'd also been the one to talk to him all those weeks ago. He handed them both the printouts that he'd brought with him.

"I want you to know that I'm impressed with your line of product and your pricing system. The receiving department is top-notch as well. The way you bring in the goods and catalog them means that anyone coming into this building can pull up a number for the product and go right to the warehouse to find where it is. You have a good team of inventory control as well." Noreen said that her father had always been a stickler for keeping things organized. "It shows in your work here. The line is good. A little outdated, but will run you for a few more years before I would recommend that you replace it. I would suggest that you put in a labeling system that also runs your lines. That way when you have a box go to the store, you can be assured that that's where it went."

"Why do I think that the 'but' you're about to tell us is going to be costly?" Mac told him not at all. "The way that Elton talked, you were disappointed in the way things were going here and that he thought you were going to tell us it was a lost cause. He seemed to think that you were under the impression that we should just close up and be done with the entire thing. We can't do that, if that's what you're going to say. Our father built this company on nothing but a handshake. If we can make it work, that's what we'll do."

"I see. You paid me to give you the truth. And I think, in detail, you were told that I'm a man that seldom beats around the bush about things. And if you can't handle that, we won't be able to work together, correct?" Again the two of them looked at each other before nodding. "All right then...you want this company to prosper and continue to be a viable company, then fire Elton. I mean, not tomorrow or next week, but today, this minute."

"Really? Elton? I mean, I know that he's sort of set in his ways, but he's been working with us since Dad died. Seriously, I don't think we could have gotten this far without him. And I know that my dad thought a great deal of him. I mean, he did have his issues with him, but he's been working here for all of our lives." Mac nodded. "I don't even know if we can fire him. I mean, he and Dad were good friends, and he's been at all our birthday parties since.... I'm sorry, Mr. Harrison, but I think you should reconsider that suggestion. He's a good man and works very hard."

"Fine." Mac stood up and gathered his things, including the paperwork that he'd given them. As he was putting everything back into his briefcase, he told them what he was going to do. "There won't be any charge for me coming here other than expenses, and my secretary will see that you're given a full accounting of —"

"Wait. I mean...you're just going to stop there? You're not going to suggest anything else for us? You were there for two weeks. Surely you had to have found the real reason for our production lines to go so slowly." Mac told them he had, it was Elton. "You mean to tell me that one man, a single man, is responsible for us losing sixty-four percent of our production time line?"

"No." Mac pulled on his jacket and picked up his things. He could tell that they were relieved, but it was going to be short lived as soon as he spoke again. He almost hated to tell them. "Elton is responsible for eighty-six percent of your slow down. And if he's not taken off the line and forced into retirement, then you will lose more every day until you fail. And you will, at the rate you're going."

Mac was nearly to the door outside when he heard someone call his name. It was Elton. Mac had had enough of the man for one day, so went out to get in the car and go home, but Elton followed him. And the man looked like he had received his Christmas bonus as well as a tax refund all in the last ten minutes. Elton walked up to him as he waited for his car and put out his hand to shake it. Mac just looked at it, then at the man he'd left hanging.

"I could have told you that they'd not do anything about me. I'm sure that you told them that it was me that was hurting things. I'm their go-to man when they need answers. And they don't know shit about what I do or what goes on down on the line, and that's the way I want it. I'm not going to let them change a damned thing, just so you know. When they fail—and I've no doubt that it'll be sooner rather than later—I will own a nice business." Mac didn't look at the couple that walked up behind Elton, nor did they speak. He did, however, ask Elton what he was talking about. "The will. I know for a fact that it states that once the business closes down that all the original members of the staff will be able to purchase the company for what the fair market value is. And when this is done, the fair market will be considerably less than what it is today, don't you think?"

"So you want this company to fail. After all the work that Mr. Stokes put into making this a valuable firm for his children, you're going to let it fail so you can take it from them." Elton smiled and nodded. "And what are you going to do with it once you own it? Call in some help and get it up and going again? That's not very fair of you, now is it?"

"Their daddy left them all the money. All of it. He didn't even consider us people who did all the work for him." Elton laughed as he continued. "There was a time I might have been willing to get things going in the right direction, but they called in professional help instead of asking me what the fuck was wrong with things. I could have told them that, don't you think?"

"You mean that you shut down the lines four times a day when you want to take a nap? That you have been known to sabotage the boxes before they were loaded on the truck so that the customers would be pissed enough to cancel orders?" Elton nodded. "I guess you have a hard heart there, Elton. Whatever will you do now?"

"Do? I won't have to do anything. They kicked your ass out, didn't they?" Mac said nothing, but he knew that

Noreen was pissed off. Bryon moved back, heading to the building. "What are you going to do, Mr. Harrison? I'm sure that this is a blow to your little company too, isn't it? Not being able to make this work for them. But I'm glad to see you leaving with your tail between your legs. It does my heart good to see another firm fail. It's what I live for."

"I think I did all right here, if you want to know the truth, Elton. Just fine indeed." His limo pulled up just as security was coming out of the building. "You, however...I don't think you're going to be cashing in on anything. You have a good day, Elton. I'm sure that things are about to look...well, differently for you."

Security was talking to Elton as his car pulled away. Mac could have gone back in, he supposed, talked to the Stokes about the rest of his findings, small things that he was sure that they would find once Elton was gone. But he wanted to go home. Now. He had a new home he was having fun in, a new sister in Riordan's wife that was working with him, and he wanted to go and see his mom and dad.

~~~

"You find her yet?" George Collins looked up at his son, Jim, and felt a twist that touched his heart. *How a man could have such an idiot for a kid*, he thought. A moron that didn't know shit from anything. He wished now after all these years that he'd taken his sister Hester's advice and just left him somewhere. Now he was too old for that shit and he was stuck with him. "That bitch that called the law on me, thinking that I had no rights to my own daughter, will be next. I don't cotton to being treated that way by nobody. You hear me?"

"Yes, sir, I've been looking. If they stowed her away, they sure ain't saying much. Aunt Hester, she's about to have ten kinds of fits over this. She said you should have taken better care not to get caught." George nodded. He sure should have. "When she comes down here, I'm telling you right now heads are going to be split if she don't get her way. She said for you to get home."

His sister, Hester Casey, was a force, she was. He loved her to the end of time, but she was a mite on the scary side when she was upset. Even when she was in a fairly good mood, he tried his best to keep away from her. George was afraid of her, plain and simple. Not just a little either; she'd beaten him so badly he almost couldn't lift up his beer when the mood struck her.

"You tell her that you got this. Tell her that I'm okay and that once we get Andi back home, we're gonna chain her to the floor like she done told us we should have months ago. She might not have any money coming in, but we'll have food cooked for us." Jim asked him how they was gonna have food if Andi didn't work. "You just let me worry on that, fool. I don't rightly know just yet, but I'll get it figured out."

Six months ago they'd had their welfare cut. Not just him, but Hester and Jim too. The government got it in their head that they had to work some for the money. Hell, if he wanted to work, he'd find him a job. But so far as he was concerned, when you start paying somebody for not working, you can't just up and take that from them. It just wasn't the way that things were done in his family.

None of them had found gainful employment yet, whatever the fuck that was, and he wasn't about to go look for it either. Not that Jim could. He was as stupid as they came. But George's family was on a protest. They weren't gonna find them a job until the government got their shit together and put things back the way they were.

George had been stuck in jail for three days now. He was getting food regular like. Not nearly as much as he wanted, but he was getting it. No beers either. They had some fool rule about that. Why a man couldn't be enjoying his leisure was beyond him. He looked up at his son and wondered if it was too late to do something about getting rid of him. Probably.

"Dad, they said you might be going back to jail, the one real far away. That having that gun was against the rules. I thought you said to me that rules don't work on us. That we was special or something." He told Jim he wasn't gonna go nowheres so long as he was breathing. "But if you do, what's gonna happen to me? I can't be living with Aunt Hester. She don't like me none. I was thinking when we find Andi I might go see if she'll let me stay with her. She's gotta be nicer to me than Aunt Hester is, don't you think?"

"Nobody likes you, son. You're stupid and you ain't worth the sex that we had to make your ass. Your momma, God rest her lazy-assed soul, she done should have known better than to birth you and that ignorant daughter. Now look at me, stuck here and nobody to help me out." George stood up and glared at his son, who backed away. "You find Andi, tell her to get her ass down here and tell them folks that she fell again. And that the gun was hers. I ain't going back to jail. I ain't, you hear me?"

After Jim left him to have another look for his sister, George thought of his lot in life. He wasn't stupid, but he was lazy. He'd admit that to anyone who asked him. And he didn't care much for his daughter or his son, but he'd been given them and he had to suffer with having them. His wife, he'd tolerated her some, but she'd given him Jim and then a useless daughter, then up and left him with them like he wanted to be taking care of them for the rest of his life. Hester…well, Hester was his big sister, and he knew better than to mess with her.

"Mr. Collins?" He nearly missed hearing his name and stood up in his cell to see who might be thinking he was a mister anything. "Are you Mr. Collins? George Collins?"

"I am. What you want? In case you missed it, if you're selling something, I ain't got me no money. If you're lawyering up for somebody, can't help you there. I don't rat out my buddies." The man said nothing. There was something about him that just told you that he was untouchable, and that had George moving back when the man walked up to the bars. "What is it you want of me?"

"I'm here to tell you that Andi Collins is off-limits to you and your family. She's in a good place, and you're to stop harassing her from now on." George just stared at the man. "And if you're caught within one foot of her, I'm going to bring a hell down on you so hard you won't be able to lift a hand to bring whatever shit food you eat to your mouth."

"You can't tell me what to do with my own kid. I know my rights. I brought her into this fucking world, and she'll do as she's told." The man said nothing. "Who the fuck do you think you are, anyways? I know she ain't bringing the law down on me. 'Cause if she can afford you, in your expensive suit, then she'd better be getting her ass down here and bailing me out. I'm her daddy, damn it."

The man only stared at him. George wanted to flip him off, his favorite pastime when things didn't go his way, but he had a feeling that if he even lifted his hand to do so, then he'd be hurting bad. Worster than he was right now.

"Stay away from her or pay the price." As the man walked away, George could feel his bravery coming back to him. But before he could open his mouth to curse at the man, he was standing in front of George with his hand around his throat, lifting him up off the floor.

The man changed. Not just his body but his face, and even his fingernails at his throat seemed to bite deep into his neck. George looked into his eyes then; they sort of captured him. The man's eyes had darkened to an almost black, and George felt his bladder just let go when he saw the fangs there on his lip.

"Stormy said that if I wanted, I could play. I might just yet anyway. Would you like that?" George shook his head. "Too bad. Go near Andi again and I will kill you. Not a threat, you dumb fucking idiot, but a promise. You know that I'm telling you the truth too, don't you, moron?"

"Yes." George wanted to cry. He knew something, a feeling of fear like he'd never felt before. "I won't bother her no more."

"Good. See that you don't." As he was dropped to the floor, the man straightened his suit sleeves and then his tie. "You might want to tell your son and that sister of yours to behave too. I'm not in the mood to have to come back out in the sunlight to wipe this family out of their miserable existence. And you'd do well to remember that if I have to come back, you will be dead. Understand me?" George nodded.

Long after the man had left him, George stayed on the floor. Lots of things were going through his mind as he lay there. The man had had fangs. He wanted to think that was just a figment of his addled head, but he had a feeling that they were as real as rain. And the man had lifted him up like he was nothing more than a bothersome flea.

George knew that he was big. Not muscled—those had never been a part of his body in any way—but just plain fat. When he was younger, he'd been heavy. As he grew, so did not only his waistline but his entire body. George figured he weighed a good four hundred pounds. And the man had lifted him up with a single hand. But the longer he lay here, just thinking and letting his mind wander, the less and less of the man he could remember.

"I gotta stay away from my daughter. I don't know why, but I gotta." Nodding to himself, he stood up. He'd pissed himself...not the first time. But this time he could almost smell the fear in his urine. "Couldn't get off the floor, that's all. Happened before, when that chair of mine wouldn't lift me right. Can't be nothing more than that."

He knew that there was something there that he had to remember besides not bothering Andi again. Fangs? Nobody had fangs except them people faking it, like he'd seen on television. He also had a feeling that he'd been flying too. But that wasn't right either, was it? Sitting on the bed, unmindful of his wet pants, he frowned. When he thought of Andi again, he felt a little pain in his head when he thought of making her ass pay, but it went away after a minute or two.

"She's gonna pay. That she is." Nodding, stretched out on the bed, he felt sticky. And when he moved around, the bed groaned. It was scary there for a minute. The bed he was using creaked a bit more than he liked. Sitting on the side of the bed, he pulled off his pants and underwear and took them to the sink. He'd get more later, but these were just stinky. Laying them on the sink, he went back to his bed. He had some thinking to do.

CHAPTER 2

Andi watched the woman—Martha Peterson, she'd been told at the counter—pour pancake batter on the grill. There was nothing to it really, but Martha was still messing it up. Keeping her hands behind her back so she'd not reach for the pitcher and do it herself, Andi thought about how grateful she was to Storm.

"You'll work there and not leave until someone comes to get you. We'll drop you off, too, when we can, or one of the staff will."

Andi had been released from the hospital the morning after her father had hurt her, and was brought to Storm's house where she got a wonderful meal and a lovely room to stay in for the night. Now she was here with a job that paid very well. Andi was as happy as she'd ever been.

There was a bakery next door, but that place gave her the willies with all the business and people coming and going. Andi didn't care that much for lots of people around. Storm had laid out what she wanted from her, and since she'd been so wonderful in not making her go home with her father, Andi would do just about anything for her. The smell of burning batter brought her from her thoughts.

"Oh my, this isn't good at all. I think this old grill has about had it, don't you? Just look at this mess. You'll have your work cut out for you if this is the way this thing is going to work for us." Andi said nothing to Martha when she asked, but decided if the orders were going to get filled she was going to have to do something.

"I can do this if you want to have a seat. I know you said your leg was hurting." Martha looked longingly at the chair, then back at the grill and told her, not for the first time, that she could not lose her job. "I think I can make it work. But if I don't, you can blame it on the new girl. Just have a seat and we'll be the only ones that know it."

"My legs sure do hurt. Old age ain't all it's cracked up to be." Andi wanted to point out she was younger than the two women in the bakery next door, and they were running around like they were half her age. "I'll just sit a spell and you see if you can make this old girl work for you."

As soon as she had all the burnt pancakes off the grill, Andi did something that she'd never done before: she pretended to be clumsy. And in doing so, spilled all the batter all over the empty sink. Her timing was perfect, she thought.

"I'll do it," Andi told Martha when she started to get up to remake the batter. "Won't be a minute. I can't believe that I've tripped up on my own feet. No harm though...I can get it fixed as good as new."

Mixing up the batter she knew from heart, Andi was pouring fresh batter on the grill in less than five minutes. Ham was next, along with bacon and sausage. The orders were piling up and she had to work fast to get them finished. As she pulled the first stack off and filled it with the sides, the waiter—Billy, his name was—had just put up another order. He looked at the platter she gave him and at

Martha without a word. When he walked away with the orders, she wondered for a second what that had been about, but was too busy to worry too much.

An hour later, Martha was still sitting at her table, but now she was barking orders at her—She was filling the plates too full; Billy would spill them. The pancakes were too big; they'd expect that every day—things like that until Andi had to tune her out or hit her. Billy came back once and told Martha that she should be helping, but she told him to fuck off. Andi was used to harsh words between people, so only worked on the things in front of her. To be honest, she was having too much fun to care what they were doing behind her.

When the breakfast rush was over, Martha gathered up her things and said she was going home. That it seemed to her that Andi had it under control until lunch. She told her to make the soup but not to screw it up, and that she'd be back at noon. And not to tell anyone where she'd gone. As she made her way to the door, she turned back to her, and Andi had a moment of unease. It was there and gone, the look on Martha's face that scared her a little.

"I can't lose my job, you know. My medicines are expensive, and I don't get much in the way of pension." Martha looked around the big kitchen and smiled. "I sure would hate to have Storm fire you for messing up this new business of hers. So you take care to do the soup right, and I won't have to tell her that it was all your fault that breakfast was such a disaster."

She left, and Andi looked at Billy when he came into the kitchen with her. He got them both a juice and told her to have a quick seat before she began again. After she thanked him, he leaned back in his seat and looked at her.

"She's going to lose her job, you know. Not because of you, but because of how she's been acting of late. I had four people say they were ready to not come by any more even if the meal is free to them if they was served those things she called pancakes any more. You made some very nice people happy today." Andi didn't know about all that, but got up and started looking for vegetables for some soup. "What do you need for me to do to help you?"

"She said I had to make some soup. But she didn't say what kind or how much." Billy asked her if she had ever made soup before. "Yes. I used to cook for my family. And for a while I was a short order cook for a restaurant down town. It's why Mrs. Harrison put me here."

"Okay, how much…. We usually get in about seventy-five for lunch on Thursday. Not all of them eat soup, but a lot of them do. Does that help?" She said that it did, then asked him where the fresh vegetables were. "If you're gonna make it from scratch and not use that canned shit, they might all eat soup today. But it's over there, in the pantry-like thing. And if you need something that's not there, Danny and I can go and get it for you. He does wash up for us and the bakery."

By the time Martha returned at ten after twelve, Andi was serving hot veggie soup with corn bread and sandwiches. Danny came over to wash up at eleven-thirty and had told her that while the restaurant was open to the public, most of their customers were vets down on their luck. As were the few people that worked for the restaurants. Having a place to have a hot meal and a place just to be social with others was about the best thing that could happen to most of these people.

"Storm is a big time vet. Honored by the president himself, I guess." Andi handed Danny a bowl of soup and he got his bread. Billy was taking the soup from the window, but she'd put the cornbread out there for him to serve up. It was a system that worked for them both. "Boy oh boy, I do like cornbread. If there be any left over, I'd sure be in a mind to take it back home with me."

Andi told him that it wasn't up to her, but she'd wrap him up a couple of pieces before she had to go for the day. He was so happy that he began to whistle a tune that made her smile. She wondered if he knew that the lyrics were dirty. *Probably*, she thought. He was a vet, too, she'd found out from Billy.

Martha was not happy with any of them when she came in. Her first order of business was to tell her that fresh vegetables were not to be made into soup, and that the food was supposed to be on this side of the kitchen, not out there with the others.

"This is a good idea, letting me get the bread for my customers, don't you think, Martha?" Billy had to have heard Martha and winked at her when he spoke. "I think I could get—"

"You just don't get used to it. I'm not going to do it for you. I'm in charge of this kitchen, not her." Martha looked over at her with a smile that didn't reach her eyes. "You don't want me to lose my job over something that won't work out too good, would you? I mean, Storm, she hired me to run this kitchen like I wanted. I thank you for giving me a break, but I'm ready to take over now."

Andi moved back from the grill. She wasn't sure what to do now, so she went to the front of the restaurant to see if she could help out there. Billy put her right to work waiting on customers at the bar. The first man she waited on looked like he was more afraid of her than she was of her dad.

"What can I get for you?" He looked at her, then dropped his eyes again. "We have veggie soup and cornbread. Can I get you some of that?"

"Please. And some milk if you have it." She told him she did and ordered him the soup and bread. While she got the milk, Billy moved by her and told her to be careful of Craig. He'd been hurt where they couldn't fix him. Taking him his bowl of soup, Andi handed him his silverware and smiled at him again. "You new?"

"Yes. Today is my first day. I hope you like the soup. I made it too." She'd never bragged on herself before but was hoping for a smile from the man. When he only bent his head over his bowl, Andi moved to the next customer.

Several times she heard Martha yell for her, and each time she'd been in the middle of helping a customer and just couldn't break away. Andi thought that if she wanted to push her out of her domain, then she was welcome to it. Besides, Andi was having a blast talking to customers, getting them what they wanted. So when everyone cleared out and Billy locked the doors, she sat down in one of the booths with him rather than going back to the kitchen. Martha came out huffing.

"You abandoned me when you're supposed to be working for me. See if I don't tell Storm that. You might just lose your job, and I don't think I care very much." Billy told her to fuck off, and Martha turned her anger on him. "I had to serve up that slop in there, and you were not helping me either pushing them orders on me when I was trying to fix that stuff she left me. I told you to take the bread back out there, and you just wouldn't do it."

"No, I didn't, did I? When you explained to me, in front of thirty people, that the kitchen and what came out of it was yours to work with, and I decided to let you deal with it and gave you the bread to deal with too. And from my understanding from Storm, Andi here is supposed to help where she is needed. She made lunch while you were napping in the car, made sure that the place was spit polished after the mess you made at breakfast, and helped me serve her food to a lot of very happy customers. Unlike the ones you normally serve with that slop—as you called it—you make up."

When she left them, telling them that she was going to call Storm right now, Andi asked Billy if she was going to lose her job. He smiled at her and told her that he doubted it very much. That when Storm asked him, and she would, he'd tell her just what had happened and what Martha had done.

"I can't go back home. Storm said that I'd not have to, but if she can't have me working here, I don't know what I'll do." Billy put his hand over hers just as someone knocked at the front door of the place.

The man standing there looked...scary was the first thing that popped into her head, and then handsome. Like the kind of handsome that made her think of sexy book covers and nights of sex and sweaty sheets. Shaking her head a little, she stood up when Billy went to the door to open it and two more men came in. Billy seemed to know them, so she went to the kitchen to see what needed to be done in there and to see if she could talk to Martha.

Martha was gone. And in her place she'd left...well, a mess would not have even covered what the kitchen looked like. And a lot of it, Andi knew, she'd done on purpose.

The cornbread pans were all over the place, most of the bread unfit to eat. Andi had made three pans of it, each of them to go in after the one before it was taken out of the oven. It looked like Martha had pulled them out, cut out the middle pieces, then dumbed the rest on the table. The vegetable pot that she'd used was also on the table. Its contents were cold now, and she wondered if she'd done anything to it. The lid to it was in the trash, as was some of the leftover soup. Martha had told them toward the end of lunch that they were out of soup, and now she knew why. That wasn't the end of her destruction either.

Dirty ladles and serving bowls had been dropped on the floor, their pottery pieces and soup smeared all over the place like she'd walked in it sliding around so that it was ground into the floor tile. Billy touched her shoulders and startled a small scream from her when he entered the kitchen behind her.

"Holy fuck." She started to cry. There was nothing tears could do about this, but she knew that Martha was going to blame it on her. "Don't move. Just…just don't move."

The door behind her opened and closed. As she moved to the table to start the cleanup, the three men that had come in a few minutes ago came in the kitchen with Bill. He was explaining what had happened today. Andi backed away from them; they were very large, strong men—even the older man.

"I'm telling you right now that if she tries to say that Andi did this, I'll quit. And you told me that if I had to quit this place that you'd close it down. This just isn't right, and you guys know it. Andi had the customers happy today. You should have seen her pancakes. Looked like fluffy bits of heaven. And tasted that good too. Even old Craig had a second bowl of her soup." Andi tried to tell them it was nothing. That she'd just done what Martha told her. "She left us too. Right after breakfast, and didn't turn up again until after lunch rush started. I'm telling you, Aedan, that woman has to go."

The first man asked her to move back from the table, he was taking pictures. After about ten minutes of pictures being taken and Billy going on about her pancakes, the men took off their coats and started helping with the clean-up. She was surprised speechless when one of them got the mop and bucket out to start putting hot water in it.

"I can do this."

The man he'd called Aedan winked at her and continued to pick up the broken pottery while the third man began piling dishes that weren't broken in the sink. Feeling out of her element, she went to the sinks and began filling the stainless steel bowls up with hot water. There was a dishwasher, of course, but there were plenty of pots to wash up too.

After about an hour the kitchen was set to rights. Not only were all the pots and pans cleaned, but the dishwasher had been run and lunch dishes were put away as well. Danny had finished up where she'd begun, and Andi had spent the better part of that hour just cleaning the big grill. It shone like a mirror when she was finally finished. She was going to help Danny put away the pots when she heard someone clear their throat.

"You think you can cook us up some lunch?" The older gentleman helped her lift the largest pot she'd ever used out of the sink and into the rinse water. "Whatever you have around, that'll be good. But I have to tell you, the rest of them are coming over too."

"Rest?" He told her that she might have as many as ten for a late lunch. "Okay. I can do that. There is some soup too. Not much, but enough for a few bowls. And I found enough to make some sandwiches if that's okay." He assured her that it would be wonderful.

She made her way to the walk-in and thought about what was in there. There were salad fixings, of course, and some vegetables, but the size of those men led her to believe that they'd want something more substantial. Like a steak or chop. Finding two dozen of the chops and some potatoes, she figured whatever was left over Martha could serve for tomorrow's special. Andi had already figured she'd not be working here after today. No one was going to believe that she'd had nothing to do with this mess.

~~~

Mac was let into the restaurant by Ennis. The two of them had been talking via their link about what had been going on here for a couple of days while he'd been gone, and he'd told him to come by the Home Cooking. Ennis said he was just on the verge of telling Storm that Martha had to go when his family told him to have a seat, food was about ready. He was glad now that she'd taken it out of their hands, apparently. Aedan sat beside him and grinned.

"You hungry?" Mac said that he could eat. "Well shit. I was hoping you said that you'd already eaten and that whatever those smells are that are coming from the kitchen would be ours. Are you sure?"

"Yes, I'm sure." He took a deep breath and could smell the aromas. "Who did you get to come in and feed us? A four star chef? Christ, that smells like heaven."

"Yeah, no kidding. Storm and Mom are helping Andi put it all on platters, and when they have it all ready, we're going to go and bring it out when they tell us. The kitchen isn't big enough for us all; and besides, we were threatened." He asked him about what. "Andi, the cook. She said that if we got in her way again, she was going to call Martha back to finish the dinner. I think that shocked her, saying something like that. She doesn't strike me as the sort of person that would say something bad about someone else. I think we all rattled her."

He could see that. They were all grown men and large. And with all seven of them there, including his dad, he thought perhaps they were about the size of a tank. Then when you added in Billy, Mom, and Storm, he could see where even the calmest person could have a time with it.

"Set the tables closer together so we can eat." Nodding at his dad, he and Aedan started shoving tables together in a long line. Dad and Riordan were putting out silverware and Darcy was filling glasses of tea. Liam and Ennis were putting out napkins and salt and pepper shakers, pulling them from other tables. "Boy, I'm telling you, I'm sure looking forward to this meal. Don't know why, but I have a feeling it's going to be about the best we've all had in a bit. At least since Caroline passed on."

His parents' old cook had died about three months ago. Caroline had been a part of his childhood all the way up until he'd left for college, baking and cooking for the household every meal and keeping them well supplied with cookies and pies when they were away. Mom and Dad were looking but had yet to find anyone to take her place. Mac thought it was because they were still missing her.

"Okay, we're ready." He looked at his mom when she came out of the kitchen with two heavy platters. Taking one of them from her, he kissed her cheek as she told him to go into the kitchen and get the other ones. "Stormy is talking with that nice young girl. She thinks this is her last day."

"Why?"

His mom only shrugged and put her platter down, following him to the kitchen after he set his on the table. He warned the others there had better be enough for him when he got back.

There was another platter of chops, a bowl of corn, and another of green beans. Corn bread was still steaming on the stove top, as well as three big bowls of fried potatoes. His mouth started to water when he thought of how many of these alone he was going to scarf down. And if Stormy didn't want this girl, whoever she was, then he'd hire her to cook for him full time. As he took some of the platters to the dining area, he saved back one of the bowls of potatoes for himself. He figured if his family got them, he'd never get even a fried onion that was in the bowl too. Before he could leave the kitchen, however, he saw them.

Storm was a beautiful woman. And he'd be the first to tell anyone who asked that he was slightly afraid of her. He knew that if asked, she'd be armed with not just a gun, but knives as well. And he also knew that she could kick his ass even though he was bigger than her. But the woman standing next to her was who had his full attention.

Fragile was the first thought that came to mind. Then delicate. Rose-like and even soft. But he also had a feeling that she could be hard, defensive, as well as protective. He stood there staring at her when he felt someone bump him from behind. He turned to look at his dad.

"That would be Andi." Mac nodded. "She and Storm are friends, and when she was hurt a few days ago, she had her brought here to hide out. I think she asked you to look in on her while she was gone. I know that Billy has been giving you reports and all, but the shit hit the fan today. I guess her family is a piece of work."

"Married?" His dad said he didn't think so, but that he'd heard from Ennis that it was a dad and aunt that were making things hard for her. "Do you think they'll come here for her?"

For some reason Mac hoped so. He tried to shake off the feeling that he needed to protect her by telling himself that she was a friend of Storm's, so he had to. But Mac found that he wanted to touch her too. Looking at his dad when he said his name, he handed him the platter of the coveted potatoes and made his way to the woman.

"Andi, this is my brother-in-law, Cormac. He goes by Mac. Like I was telling you, they're not going to let anything happen to you." Mac shook his head and looked at the bruising on Andi's face as Storm continued. "Come on out and have lunch with us, and let them tell you how wonderful your meal is. I'm sure that any one of them will beg you to marry them so that you'll cook for them."

The low growl coming from his throat startled all three of them. Storm cocked a brow at him and Andi backed up. He tried to reason with his cat that things were fine, but he wasn't too happy right now. Mac took a step back too and smiled at Andi.

"I'm hungry, that's all. And I guess we're all waiting on you to join us." Andi just stared at him. "Dad said that he had some of your pancakes this morning and that they were as light as feathers. And my favorite food of all time is fried potatoes."

"They were fast." He had no idea what that meant. Mac didn't venture into the kitchen except to pick up a snack or to microwave leftovers from some restaurant he or one of his brothers might have been to. He was not a cook. "You should go eat, while things are hot."

Hot. Heat. Mac felt his mind go into overdrive at the thoughts that the words brought up in his head. Not for food, though he thought of filling his belly with something, but it was the woman, not food. She must have sensed something, because she took another step back and he took one toward her this time. Storm moved between her and him. He wanted to snarl at her, but the look on her face had him pause.

You're scaring her, you idiot. Back the fuck up. He didn't want to back up and he was pretty sure that Storm knew it. *Back up or I swear to you I will shoot your dick off and slap you around with it. Back the fuck up, Mac.*

He did. One step, then another until his cat was snarling at him. Storm didn't move, didn't let him see Andi either. Mac knew that he'd frightened Andi. He felt horrible about that, but something was wrong here and he didn't understand it.

"Storm? Mac? Are you guys coming to eat?" He turned to his mom, trying to get his fuzz-filled head to reason with his body and cat. "Mac? Are you all right?"

"Yes." Even his voice wasn't right. He turned then, looking at his mom, and then nodded at her. "We're just coming now. Storm is trying to talk Andi into coming with us."

"Well of course she will." His mom came into the kitchen and wrapped her arms around Andi, pulling her past him and to the door. She was telling her how much she was looking forward to the meal she'd made when Mac turned back to Storm. She looked as pissed off as he felt confused.

"What the hell is wrong with you? I told you to back off. She's been going through some shit, and you being a fucking jackass is not going to help her." He nodded and told her he didn't know what was wrong with him. "Well, fucking straighten up or I'll make you. Do you understand me? She's got enough shit on her plate without you acting like one of her family members."

"Her aunt and father." Storm told him that if she had her way, she'd shoot them both and bury them in the back yard for the worms to get ill over. "They're hurting her for what reason?"

"They've got it in their head that she's their maid and payday all wrapped up in a pretty little bow. When I found her the other day, that piece of shit father of hers was dragging her around by her hair and telling me that she had to send him her checks. He's in jail. I had Mason go and pay him a visit, and he's supposed to not bother her again. We'll see. Mason said the man was too stupid to take to the compulsion very well, that he didn't expect him to stay away. But he'd go back and visit him a couple more times just to make sure."

"He will. Not bother her, I mean. Neither her father nor her aunt will get near her if I can help it." Storm said nothing but stared at him. "We should go eat. I mean, I'm hungry, aren't you?"

"I am. What was that?" He told her he honestly had no idea. "Well curb it, buddy, or I will. She's my friend, and I don't want you going all macho shit stupid on her."

"You have such a way with words. You know that, don't you?" Storm told him to fuck off. "Yeah, like a delicate flower you are. It's small wonder that they don't have you teach kindergarten or something like that. You'd be such a hit with the parents."

They made their way to the dining area and Mac was trying his best to get his thoughts in a row. While he'd been in the back rooms, Storm's aunts had shown up to eat with them, and he was glad for that. They were a family too, after all. Sitting down, he noticed that Andi was at the other end of the table from him, and for some reason that made him feel pissy again. But Storm grabbed his leg under the table and dug her nails — more likely her cat claws — into his thigh, and he sat still. He didn't move, thankful that she'd not gone any higher on his leg.

Mess this up and I will make that pretty face of yours look like raw meat. He nodded and put his hand over hers to remove it. But she dug deeper. Mac moved his hand and sat still until she removed hers. He didn't think he wanted to ever sit near her again at the table. Storm was not a nice person when she was being protective. He hated to see what she would be like with her own children.

CHAPTER 3

Andi was trying her best not to eat very much because she was afraid of getting ill. But they all, everyone around her, kept shoving food on her plate. And when she protested that she'd eaten earlier, no one seemed to care. She had two chops and a mound of potatoes on her plate — which would feed her entire family at home — before she had any opportunity to pass the platters beyond her. Well, her dad could eat this much and more. He'd eat this as a snack.

"Are you enjoying working here?" Nodding at Mr. Harrison, she told him she loved it, but wasn't sure if she was going to continue. "And why not? I'm telling you right now, if you cooked like this every day, there wouldn't ever be an empty seat in this place. This is amazing."

"It's just potatoes and pork chops." He laughed, and she felt her face heat up. "That other woman — Martha — she said that she's in charge of the kitchen and that she was going to talk to Storm about me. I think she made that mess you helped me clean up to show her that I'd done it. I promise you that I didn't do anything to her other than my job."

Mrs. Harrison laughed as she spoke. "We all know that, even Storm does. And Martha said that to her. Right before we got here, Martha called Stormy and told her that you had this fit, and that you had completely messed up her kitchen. That'd you'd broken her things and that she would not work with you again. That you needed to be fired. Stupid woman." Mrs. Harrison handed her a thick slice of cornbread, and Andi took it as the older woman continued. "She has no idea that my husband and sons were here when she left, and that Stormy knows that you had nothing to do with it. I'm thinking that you're going to be in charge soon. Oh, and Billy — Billy Richards — he's the manager of this place, also a doctor. He comes here, waits tables, to get to know the men and women that come in to see if they need him. It's been working well for all of them, I think."

"I see." She really didn't, but glanced down the long table at the man that had scared her. He was looking right back at her, and no matter how hard she tried Andi couldn't seem to pull her eyes from him. And when one of his brothers spoke to him and he looked at them, Andi bowed her head and let out a long breath.

"He's very handsome, isn't he?" Andi looked at Mrs. Harrison when she spoke low to her. "Stormy told me what happened in the kitchen. I guess we should have expected it to happen soon."

"Happen? What happened?" When she only smiled at her, Andi looked down the table at Mac again. But she saw a movement out of the corner of her eye that had her looking at the door. Her brother. Andi stood up when he pounded on the door.

"I have to go." Everyone stood as well, and she noticed in a vague sort of way that Storm had a gun and so did the man seated next to her. They didn't raise them up, but they looked like they could at a second's notice. "I have to go now. It's my brother, and he's going to come in here."

"Like hell he will." When she turned to move toward the back door, Mac was suddenly in front of her. Backing away from him was impossible with the table behind her, and he managed to wrap her up in his arms before she could tell him to stop. "Come on, we'll go out the back and Storm and Riordan will take care of him."

"He wants me. And he'll stop at nothing to get me if that's what Dad told him to do. Jim is…he needs to do what he's told or he gets into trouble." Mac only laughed. As she was led through the kitchen to the back door, she heard the front door open and Storm talking…well, *talking* wasn't the term she would have used, but yelling at Jim. "I have to go or he'll catch me."

"He's not going to touch you. No one is."

He was dragging her to a car…a sleek, expensive-looking car…and she was in the passenger side and buckled in before she could protest. When Mac got in on the other side, he started the car and turned to back out. But he only stared at her.

"I'd like to kiss you right now."

"Me?" He nodded, his arm still on the back of her seat, his other hand on the steering wheel. "Do you think that it'll make my brother go away or something? Because I'm pretty sure that it won't. Make him go away. Jim has problems that he can't help, and he's afraid of our dad."

"I'm sorry, but I don't give a good fuck about your brother right now. But I really would like to kiss you. If you're worried about your brother coming out here and interrupting us, I'm pretty sure that he's been detained by my family. Which gives me plenty of time to pursue the idea of tasting you." She backed from him, and he laughed. "I thought that was what you'd say. For now anyway."

He backed out of the parking space and was on the road before she could think of a reply to what he'd said. There was something very off about the man, and she wasn't sure he was right in the head. Andi thought of him growling earlier and wanted to ask him to do that again. It had warmed her in ways not even standing over the register at home had ever done.

It occurred to her that she should have asked him where he was taking her. Or at the very least why she was being taken away in the first place. Her brother wasn't a nice person, but he'd only ever hurt her when he'd been told to. He'd do what Dad told him to do to her, but he'd never do anything on his own. That didn't mean she wasn't afraid of Jim; she was. But her father was a real bastard to her and would cause her a world of hurt when he could. Her aunt too. Now there was a monster.

"Do you know anything about shifters?" The question caught her off guard and she asked him what he meant. "You know, shifters. Like a man that can be another thing, a cat in this scenario. Or even a vampire or anything that people, humans, don't believe in."

Andi looked out the window and thought of how to answer him. Was he making fun of her? There was no reason to believe that he knew about her encounter with a wolf. Her father and brother had beaten her when she'd tried to tell them about the wolf man. Glancing at Mac, she wondered what he was going to do if she admitted it.

"I don't know what you're talking about. I'd very much like it if you were to let me out of your car so I can find a place to hide." He didn't slow to stop but kept driving at a speed that was making her heart race a little. And not necessarily in a bad way. "Why do you ask me such a question? Do you mean to make fun of me? Hit me if I tell you what you don't want to hear?"

"No. I have no intentions of hitting you, ever. And I won't make fun of you. If you've some knowledge of what a shifter is, then this will make things a little easier when I have to explain something to you. Something that I only just figured out on my own." She asked him what that was. "That you are my mate."

Mate. She'd heard the term before. And what it meant. She would belong to him. Not just him, but whoever he wanted to sell her to. Andi reached for the door handle, thinking that rolling from a moving car would be better than being passed around like a napkin at a banquet hall.

"Don't do that." He reached for her hand just as she touched the handle. "Please, just listen to me and I'll explain."

"I don't need you to explain. I know what mate means. My friends at school, they told me what happens when you become a mate to men. And what they didn't tell me, my father and aunt explained the rest. Mates use you, and then when they've had enough, they pass you around to all the other men they know. I won't have it."

The car suddenly stopped. Her seatbelt cut into her neck, and she nearly hit her head on the dash it stopped so abruptly. Mac turned to her after shutting down the car, and she whimpered when he reached for her.

"I won't hurt you. I won't share you. Who the fuck were you talking to? Not another shifter, that's for sure. We don't pass around our mates. And we certainly don't beat them. We can't. Ever. Our kind treasures our mates, not…. I'd really like for this conversation to be made when we're sitting down." She looked at the seat, then back at him.

"Okay, sitting in my home on furniture so that we can talk about this calmly."

"I want you to take me back to the restaurant. I'd rather deal with Jim than...you're not my mate." He growled again, and before she could appreciate the feelings he gave her, he pulled her to him and kissed her.

~~~

Mac had only meant to hold her in his arms, talk to her calmly, and explain. But the moment he touched her, put his hands on her skin, all he could think about was tasting her. Having her naked over him, under him, he didn't care at that moment. But himself deep inside of her was all he wanted right now. As he deepened the kiss, pulled her body over his as he let the seat go back as far as it would go, Mac knew that he was going to have to slow things down. He could taste her innocence on her like perfume.

"I need to stop this." He heard the words leave his mouth, but his hands and body had other things they wanted to do. Her blouse was lifted up, her breasts bared for him. Just a taste, he told himself. He only wanted to suckle at her breast, to taste her.

"Please. Don't." He wanted to heed her words but her fingers curled at the back of his head had him pulling her ass to his groin so she could feel his cock. As she rode him with his help, Mac bit down on her nipple hard enough to bring a cry from her mouth and make her body shudder in pleasure. Lifting his head to look at her, he could see the need in her eyes.

"Come for me, Andi. Come on me like this so I can taste it on your skin." He held her to him, his cock burning to take her, his cat snarling at him to do it too. But as she rode him, her hips moving faster and faster, Mac knew that he needed more from her. All of her. When she continued to hold him to her body, he took her breast into his mouth again and, reaching between them, he freed his cock.

He needed relief. Even if he only came on her, he knew that his cat would be happy and he'd not ache so desperately to have her. But as soon as her fingers brushed over his highly sensitive cock, he tore his mouth from her breast and laid her over the seat.

"I need you. Now." Her head was nodding even as he pulled her pants off. He moved over the bucket seat, careful of the shifter between them. Lifting her up as he did, Mac tore the remains of her blouse off. Taking her breast into his mouth, he knew that he was going to hurt her.

The ability to slow his need, even for a second to breathe, was taken away from him when she nipped at his throat, bringing out his inner beast. He lifted her body up over his and slammed her down over his burning cock.

Her scream of pain tore at him. Mac held her to him, her body tightening around him so prettily that he knew even if she begged him to, there was no way for him to leave her body. Holding her, whispering in her ear how sorry he was, Mac felt like he'd ripped at his own heart to hear her crying like she was.

"I'm so sorry, baby. I didn't mean for this to happen." Andi sobbed that he did too. "Okay, I did, but not right now. I only wanted to talk to you. Kiss you a few times. Maybe even taste you, but not in my car. This is not what I wanted when I asked to kiss you."

Her head lifted and he could see the anger there. Embarrassment too, but she was spitting fire at him and he felt his cock stretch. Christ, he thought her beautiful before, but in her anger, she was gorgeous.

"Are you saying that this is my fault, that I somehow lured you into taking me in your car like this?" He shook his head, wanting to smile at her and tell her that he was enjoying this, but he was pretty sure she would hurt him. "I told you several times to take me back there, and now look at us."

He did. Looked down his body and hers to see how they were bonded. His cock was buried deep within her, her pussy wrapped around him like open arms. Moving his hips, just to see if he could go deeper, she moaned and he watched her face. When her eyes fluttered closed when he moved again, he cupped her bare ass and pulled her closer to him.

"I want to see you come like this, riding me." Her head shook, but her body was stretching for his. "I never thought this was your fault. But I'm glad that we're here. You have no idea how beautiful you look for me right now. Your pretty pussy wrapped up around me, your clit peeking out of those lips of yours. I love the way your breasts pink up, your pert nipple begging me to suckle at it. I want to do that, Andi. Do it until you come on me."

"I've never done this before." He told her he knew that. "Please. I can feel it coming, something so good, but you're not giving it to me. Help me get it, and then you can take me home."

"I'll take you home, Andi. When you come for me I'll take you home. I'm going to fill you, too, when you come." Her body seemed to jerk at his words, and he leaned in and took just the tip of her nipple in his mouth and chewed on it before looking up at her again. "You taste so delicious. So good. I can't wait to have your cum in my mouth, your pussy filing me when I eat you."

She came apart then. Her back bowed, her breasts pressed against his face, and he took one in his mouth and bit down on it, drawing blood. She came again for him, and her screaming out her release made his cock fill. Drinking from her, watching her face as she came again, he wondered if there was ever anything more beautiful than his mate coming. Pulling her mouth to his neck, leaning over for her, he told her to bite him, to mark him. When her teeth scraped over his flesh, Mac felt his balls fill painfully, his cock stretch once again. And when she bit down, not hard enough to draw blood but enough to bring him, Mac cried out and bit her on the shoulder when she came with him.

Mac held her while they got their hearts beating normally again. Christ, he'd just taken his mate in the front seat of his car and had never been happier. He was going to have to get a bigger car now, he thought. When he chuckled a little, she lifted her head and looked at him. Mac pushed her damp hair out of her eyes and looked at her.

"You're beautiful." When she started to move, he felt his cock fill again. When she froze over him, her eyes wide in shock, he smiled at her. "I'm not going to hurt you again. But I'd very much like for you to ride me again."

"I didn't say you would hurt me, but we're not going to do this again. And don't call me beautiful. I know that you think you have to after what we did, but I don't expect you to want to do this again." He asked her why not. "Because...well because of what you are and what I am."

"And what might I be or you be that would make it so that we don't make love again?" She struggled again, and he pulled her body to his, holding her tightly before she hurt either of them. "What are you thinking, Andi? About us?"

"You have all kinds of money." He didn't say anything, not even sure what to say to her. "I mean, look at this car. It worth more than I made over the last five years. Your parents are...well, nice. You have brothers that love you. While me, I don't have a pot to pee in, and after they find out what we did here, they're for sure going to fire me."

"You have to do better than that, love. My parents are nice, thank you for that. Yes, my brothers love me and I love them. As for your pot, we have a very lovely toilet at the house you can use, and no one is going to fire you for what we did. They might erect a monument in your honor, but they won't fire you." He handed her the tattered remains of her shirt. "If you can reach over the seat there, I have a bag back there with some of my clothing in it. I'll give you a shirt to pull on."

As soon as she reached for it, he knew his mistake. Or perhaps not a mistake, but an opportunity. Taking her breast into his mouth again, he rocked her over his cock up and down as he suckled at her. When her fingers curled around his shoulder, he fucked her this way, lifting her up and down so that his crown filled her over and over. Mac watched as he filled her, saw his cock, hard again, shine with her cream as it moved in and out of her.

"I could come this way. Watching you take me like this." He moved her faster, deeper, until he had her down over him once again and he was fucking her hard by bringing her tighter and tighter to him. "What I wouldn't give to have you spread out on my bed, my mouth sucking on your clit while you came for me. Come Andi. Come now."

This time he came with her. Her arms tightened around his, her mouth at his throat again. Using a little of his cat, he formed a long claw and cut at his throat for her. When Andi put her mouth over the wound and sucked on it, Mac bit down on her shoulder and came hard as blood, hot and thick, filled his mouth again.

He'd never come so hard in his life. Stars and darkness filled his vision as he emptied not once but twice more deep inside of her. When she cried out for the third time, her climax taking her, he held her tightly to him as she rode him through another mind-blowing release.

Mac held her after she sobbed herself to sleep in his arms. He'd not been able to understand what she was saying for the most part. He was a mistake—that, or she was. Something about her father and an aunt named Hester. She claimed that she was going to be killed one minute and that she was going to run far away the next. Jabber, he supposed, wasn't supposed to make much sense. When Riordan touched his mind, he was almost glad for it.

Where the fuck are you? I thought you were taking her to Mom's house. Did something happen? He said that it did. *Well, do you need for someone to come and get you? I told you that car was a mistake. You need something that isn't going to get you killed.*

I claimed her. Andi is my mate. He could almost see the look on his brother's face. It would be shocked, his eyes wide with it. And he'd be smiling so big right now that Mac would want to smack the shit right out of him. *So, if it's all the same to you, I'd just as soon you not come and get us right now.*

You made love to your mate for the first time in that car? His voice, even in his head, sounded like he was incredulous. *Mac, there is barely enough room for you in that sucker. You took her in that?*

Yeah, well, I'm sure you understand when the mood comes over you, it matters little where you are. Remember me nearly catching you in the pantry a few days ago? Riordan said nothing in reply. *I'm taking her to my house. I don't have anything here for her to wear, so I think that's the best thing. Do you know if she has some clothing that I can pick up?*

Storm said she had only the clothing on her back when she brought her home from the hospital, and has been wearing something of hers since. Well, that explained why she smelled like Storm. *I don't know what to tell you about that. Her brother, however, I have plenty to tell you. I thought Storm was going to kill him today. But he's not right in the head. I don't mean that in a cruel way, but I think he might have a developmental problem that makes him sort of slow.*

She was saying something about her aunt and her father, but little about him. I guess her dad is in jail, right? And there was mention of an aunt that might want to kill her too. Mac looked down at the bundle in his arms. *I have a mate. I mean, holy shit, Riordan, I have a mate, and she's beautiful.*

Yeah, I know that feeling. He supposed his brother would. *I think Mom knows what's going on between you two. She just asked me if you were going to take her to your house or bring her back here to our house. That's where we are by the way, at my house.*

When Andi stirred and looked at him, he told his brother that he'd talk to him later. Andi asked if she could get the clothing now. Nodding, he tried his best not to taste her again, but couldn't resist planting a small kiss on her bruised nipple. He moved over to his side of the car when she held the bag in front of her like a shield.

"I'm very sorry." When she nodded at him and looked at her feet, he thought that she'd taken that wrong and lifted her face to look at him. "Not about making love to you either time, but that your first time was in a car and not in a big bed with sheets and pillows."

"It's all right." He let her pull his shirt over her head before he pulled her to him again. She looked slightly afraid, but he knew that he'd never hurt her; no one would. "Please, you have to let me get dressed before someone comes by."

"I don't care. Look at me please." When she finally lifted her head and looked at him, he could see the tears filling her eyes. "Are you hurting? Did I hurt you too badly when I took you?"

Her face heated up when she shook her head no. "I'm fine. I'd like to go home now. You said you'd take me there. Storm said that I could stay at the apartment above the restaurant for a few days."

"I'm taking you to my house. Our house, I mean." He watched her face and knew when she realized what he said. "You don't have to be afraid of me. But I would really like to talk to you about a few things. First and foremost, your idea about mates trading around. We don't do that."

"What are you?" Her words were soft and he was pretty sure that she wasn't asking him if he was a cat, but some strange man who was different to her. But he answered her truthfully. "A cat. A tiger. You expect me to believe that you're a shifter cat?"

"I am. All my family is." He put out his arm for her and let his cat take it. "He wants to mark you, by the way. Take you in a way that has him drinking from your pussy and then marking you. Like I have. Then I want to do that as well, fuck you properly after I've eaten you until I'm full. Which I have to tell you, might not ever happen."

"You can't mean that." But her fingers moved along his arm, and he could feel his cat purring at her. "It's soft. I thought...I have no idea what I thought. How did you do that?"

"I'm a tiger. A pureblood shifter tiger." Her fingers moved over his fur again, and when she ran her cheek over it, he let more of his cat go so that she could hear him purring. "You're making him nuts to come out and play with you. You're his mate too, you know, and he wants his mate as much as I do."

She snatched her hand back and he reached for it again. Putting it back on his arm, he told his cat that they had to be gentle with her, that she was afraid of them. His cat seemed to understand and purred again, this time low enough that she didn't hear him.

"I don't know what's going on." He nodded. He had a lot of questions as well. "Will you...I don't think I want to stay with you. I do, but I don't think we should, do you?"

"Yes. I want to take you to my house, strip you down, and then make love to you until neither of us can stand up. Then when I've had my fill, in about a month, I'd like to start over again, running my tongue all over every inch of you." Her eyes dilated, her breathing picked up. Even her heartrate doubled. Leaning into her mouth, being as careful as he could, Mac kissed her before going back to the steering wheel and holding it tightly. "Right now we have to get to my house. And if you even touch me right now, which I want you to in the worst possible way, I'm going to shift, and let my cat feast on you for as long as he wants."

"Oh."

He laughed. It was that or sob. And he was pretty sure that she'd understand him less if he did that. Starting the car up, he watched her as she put her legs, bare now of anything, on the floor in front of her. Mac tried his best not to think that she was naked under his shirt, and that if he wanted, he could pull over, shift, and take her against the side of the car several times before he was satisfied. If he ever was.

CHAPTER 4

"They weren't going to kill me, but they weren't helping me find her either. And there was Andi running out with this man like she was running away from me." Jim paced the big room, avoiding the trash as he went. His dad was still in jail and might be for a little while longer. He was sorta enjoying him not being there. Aunt Hester was still there, but she was the only person he could talk to about how those people had made him feel. She wasn't really nice to him about it either, not like the Harrisons were. After a bit they'd even given him some food. He knew it was his sister's cooking too. He'd eaten everything on his plate, but he'd been scared while doing it.

"She's gotta get her ass back here. The house is going to ruin and there ain't a soul here to clean it up. And the phone bill is due too. That lady called here on it today telling me to get the promised payment in." Aunt Hester nodded as she continued. "She's gonna have a lot to answer for when she gets her skinny ass back here. Never would have been treating us like this if your daddy had done what I told him to do over and over and just tie her to the floor." He was thinking that wasn't right but said nothing to her about his feelings on that. "I know that her extra money was helping out, but that ain't worth a hill of beans if there is nobody here to wait on me. I deserve to be waited on, Jim. I'm the oldest in this family."

Jim didn't say anything to her. He'd never understood how being the oldest had gotten her any more special treatment. He was the older of he and Andi, but nobody cared about that. He missed his sister, and if he was honest about it, he was glad that she'd gotten away from here. Aunt Hester would kill her if she was still here. It was hard on Jim, but his sister was all right and that was important to him. Always had been.

"Do you think you can go down and see if those fellers want to buy your sister from us for about a week? I'm betting that one or two of them would like a good fuck with her. Course, they can't keep her, but they can have some fun with her for a little bit." Jim didn't have a clue what she meant and asked her about it. Sell her? Aunt Hester told him what she meant as she continued about the selling part. "How much you figure it would be worth to them to fuck her? If they want, they can even play rough with her too. Ain't like she's never been beaten before a few times."

"I don't think that's right. We can't sell her to them. What if they hurt her or something? I seen it on the news, Aunt Hester. We can't be selling my sister. There are laws about that." Jim frowned as he thought of something. "Those people have guns. I don't know why they pulled them on me, but I seen them. I was only trying to get Andi to get her ass home like Dad said for me to do."

"She's ungrateful. All this time we've let her do her own thing, and this is how she repays us. I told your father not to let her get by with this. Having a job and going to school like she did. What did she think that education was going to get her? A man?" Aunt Hester snorted. "She's not no more going to get a man than I am. And let me tell you, I had all kinds of them when I was younger."

Jim tried to imagine that, and just couldn't. His aunt wasn't what he'd call courtable. She wasn't even what he'd call someone he would think of as even remotely pretty. She was plain. And fat. And dirty. And she stank up the house when she took off her shoes. Jim said none of these things because, like any sane man, he was terrified of her. Like he figured any normal person would be if they had to live with her.

Aunt Hester had killed a man. This was not a story that he'd heard growing up. It wasn't something that he'd heard as a rumor, either. He'd seen her do it. Just plucked the man right out of his car when he'd come to collect on something and snapped his neck. When he didn't move any more, she dropped him on the ground and kicked him in the head.

"You got something to say to me?" Jim was shaking his head at her even before she finished asking him. "Then you get on over there at that place where you seen her and see if they'll buy her for a week. I think you should get about five hundred for her. She's got a pretty enough face, I guess, but nothing on her body that many men would want. You get going, and don't you dare think to spend any of my money before you get back here either."

He left then. There was nothing holding him there, he told himself, not even any scraps of food to eat, and his belly was growling for it again. He'd seen what those people had been eating, and he was sure that his belly had told him that he'd been hungry. Chops and green beans, like they was having some sort of feast. It had been so long since he'd had real food, he'd been thinking that they must be the luckiest people in the world right then, and he'd been given some of it before they told him to go away and not come back. Course, he'd known that Andi was a good cook. When she'd been working in the restaurant before this one, she'd sneak him food out near the back door and let him eat it. Andi would take care of him when Dad didn't have him some assignment to go after her. He didn't know what to do when he was supposed to bring her home, so he just ate his food and forgot about the rest. Andi was good to him most of the time, but he knew that she was afraid of him too.

Jim had to walk to town. Two days ago he'd run out of gas in his truck and there hadn't been anyone to bring him any, nor was there money for him to even get enough to try to get back to the house. He'd have to see about draining a car in town again, then walking back to where he'd parked it. Jim wondered if that man he was supposed to talk to about selling Andi to him would give him enough extra to fill up his tank.

By the time he got back to town, it was getting dark. The restaurant, called Home Cooking, was closed up; all the lights inside were off too. The bakery next door to it had some lights on, but he didn't go there. The last time he'd tried to get into that place, he'd nearly had his ass shot off. What the heck was going on with everyone having a gun lately? He moved to the street behind the Bakery and sat against the opposite wall watching and waiting. Maybe they'd toss out the day old stuff and he'd have enough to eat now and then in the morning before he had to see his dad again.

Jim thought about his family while he was sitting there. His dad was a mean man and had been his entire life. Jim knew that he blamed his mom on what had happened to him when he'd been born. Jim had heard him screaming at her when she'd been big with Andi that she'd better not fuck this boy up like she'd done before. His mom would sit and cry about it, telling him that it wasn't his fault but that of his birth. Jim hadn't understood that either. But when she'd told him that she was having him a little sister and not to tell his dad, she'd told him that he'd have to be the one to watch over her, that no one else would. She'd been right about that too.

"Then she up and died, my momma did." Jim missed her more and more every day. She'd been good to him, protecting him when she could. She'd told him that taking things that didn't belong to you was bad, but his dad had beaten him when he told him that and Jim had had to steal. Jim knew that stealing would get you arrested and had said that to his dad.

"No, we're not stealing a damned thing. What we're doing is making the system work for us. When the government fails, and it will, we'll still be able to feed ourselves because we know how to do it right." Jim had nodded, but he really didn't understand him. "You just do what I tell you to do and I won't have to kill you. Even though it pains me to have you breathing."

"But Mom said not to do it." His dad had cuffed him hard enough on the chin that it still hurt him to this day if he opened his mouth too wide. Jim learned really fast not to disagree with him when his dad was close enough to hit him again.

"We can work the system, like I said. We know how to make a living on the backs of others, get in and out of places that nobody thinks we can, and we can hide out where nobody will ever find us when we need to." All things that Jim thought were not right. But like with his aunt when she spouted off about how they were good citizens just trying to get by, he kept his mouth shut.

His questions might have been something like, what is this system that you talk about? And if there is one, what system are we going to be working to live if it fails? If we can get in and out of a place without keys or permission, how is that not breaking and entering? And hiding out? Wasn't that evading? Jim wasn't smart, nor did he have a good thinking process, but he'd been arrested for these things. B&E, theft, as well as evading the cops when they come looking for him. So he knew these things at least enough to know that he wasn't to do them and get caught again. And twice when he'd done that, his aunt had ratted him out.

Aunt Hester had come to live with them after her husband had passed away. Jim was about five, he thought, and Andi had been just a wee little baby. His mom, sick when she'd gotten big with his sister, had died soon after she'd come home from the hospital.

And right from the get go, Aunt Hester had hated Andi. Pinching her when she thought no one was looking. Keeping her food from her for no good reason other than she just did it. There were times when Jim would get up on the middle of the night just to sit at the bottom of her crib to keep his aunt from going into her room and smothering her, as she had said she would do on several occasions when Andi would cry for her food.

His dad wasn't a good man either when it came to Andi. He never did once hold her when she cried, and after a little bit, Jim was glad for it. He was afraid that he'd do what he said and bash her little head against the wall to get rid of her.

George Collins had been in prison twice, once for a robbery that he'd taken a gun to, and then when he'd gotten home from that, he'd been arrested again and sent away for the same dumb thing. Aunt Hester had been in charge of them then, and Jim had had to work real hard then at keeping them both from harm. Then Andi had gotten out and got a job. But nothing stopped his dad from hurting her then either.

Jim thought maybe his dad should have been using his own money for bills and stuff instead of making Andi give over her checks. Even their aunt had a check coming in every month to cover her expenses, and she made sure that he knew they were *her* expenses too. He also knew for a fact that they had one of them welfare cards. But according to their dad, the government had decided that if he didn't work, he didn't get it. And that had set him off quickly enough that Jim had left to hide out until his temper cooled or the government saw the error of their ways, as dad called it.

Jim wondered if he just stayed away if it would be safe for Andi too. Neither of them seemed to be able to find her like he did. Of course, his dad had that one time, and look where it got him. In county where Jim thought he belonged anyway. But his aunt, so far as he knew, never left the house but to get her check and to shop for her things. Jim had never seen her in any other—

"You lost?" Jim looked up at the woman in front of him. He'd been sitting there thinking for so long that he'd missed the possible trash dumping and maybe something to fill his belly, he just knew it. "I asked you a question, Jim. Are you lost?"

"I'm not a good person." He didn't look away from the woman. He knew who she was, or at least where he'd seen her before. It was the woman with the gun from today. "I'm just hungry and was waiting on the trash to be taken out. I didn't bother nobody. Even though Aunt Hester told me to find Andi and make her come home, I'm not going to do it. Not anymore."

She didn't say anything for several minutes, and Jim stood up. He didn't want to die here in this alley, and he was pretty sure that she'd do it just to get him out of her way. Before he took two steps, she told him to wait. He turned to look at her, just knowing that she was gonna be pointing a gun at him. When she wasn't, he felt his breath whoosh out of his body.

"We don't keep the leftovers at either place of business, so there wouldn't have been any food for you. They're taken to the shelter for them to use." He nodded. Of course they did that. It was a good thing to do, and here he was thinking to steal it. "Come on with me and I'll see that you get something to eat."

"I'm Andi's brother." She told him she knew. And then told him her name. "Mrs. Harrison, I don't want no trouble, if you don't mind. I been sitting here thinking, and I know you could just kill me now and not one person might care about it. But if you'd see to Andi, keep her safe, I'd be right fine with that happening to me."

"Yeah, I would though. Care, I mean. I don't kill men because they're cold and hungry. And Andi is safe." She moved with him to the car sitting on the street. There was a big man standing there, the guy from earlier that had a gun too. Jim paused and the woman laughed. "This is my husband, Riordan. And if you call me Mrs. Harrison again, I might hurt you. He's Riordan and I'm Storm. Got it?"

"Yes. Are you going to take me to jail? My dad's there and he'd be powerfully mad at you...well, he is already, but he'd be mad at me too if you do that." She asked him why she'd do that. "Because you told me to stay away from this place. But to be honest with you, I kinda wish that you wouldn't take me to jail but to the other place. Prison. Just don't let them put me next to my dad when he's taken back. He's...I've been thinking."

"Thinking is good so long as it's not going to get you killed. And that stunt you pulled this morning wasn't smart and could have gotten you just where you want to be." He got in the back seat of the car and waited while they got in the big limo with him. Storm turned to him when she was buckled. "We're going to help you right now, Jim. But if you fuck up, I will snap your neck like a twig and leave your sorry ass by the side of the road for the buzzards to pick over."

"Yes, ma'am." Jim felt tears fill his eyes. His father would have slapped him or taken a belt to his back. Not for what he'd done but because he'd been caught at it. "I don't want to do this no more. I don't want to be hungry or hurting either. I don't want to hunt down Andi and bring her back to that place. It's evil there. I'm evil."

Riordan looked at him then. The man had been quiet until that moment. "You want to make a turn in your life?"

"Yes, sir, I do. I really do. I'm not sure what my aunt will think about that. I'm not...I've spent some time in jail. Stealing and stuff. I could tell you that they made me. Had me go in and take that stuff so they could they could get paid by some other guy who wanted it. But I did it no matter what was said. I've been mean to Andi. She...never once did she call me dumb or stupid when we were together. She is a good girl. I watched her as best I could, but Dad, he's hurtful when he don't get his way, and sometimes I'd have to do what he said."

"She's marrying my brother soon. I guess that makes us sort of related." Jim nodded. He felt a little jealous of her, not angry as he probably should have, and he only nodded again. "You can come and work for me."

Jim was sure that he'd not heard him right. He knew this man and his family. Not actually them but their name. The Harrisons, their name always told you they were good people. Jim asked him what he meant by working for him.

"I don't want to do nothing bad no more. I...you should know, too, that I'm not right in the head. My momma hurt me when...Dad said that she tried to kill me before I was born. Mom said it wasn't nobody's fault, but Dad kept at me. Not sure what he meant by that so I asked somebody. The cord thing, it got all tangled up around me and I got hurt that way. My dad said I'm just four cents shy of a nickel."

"Your father is a fucking bastard." Jim was nodding before he could think he should disagree with Storm. "You'll work for us, and if I hear you tell someone else that you're not right in the head and your mother did it, I will...I will not make you happy with me."

"Yes, ma'am." He grinned then, thinking her the most wonderful woman he'd ever met. "You just tell it like it should be, don't you? I like that. I mean, I guess you can be mean when you wanna, but I'm betting people know when you're pissed off."

Riordan laughed and Storm punched him in the arm. Jim didn't think they were angry with each other, just...he thought they were just playing around. When the big car stopped, he felt his belly cramp up. He just knew right then and there, he was going to jail.

~~~

Riordan was reminded of a dog that had been beaten so much that he wasn't going to trust his own paw to scratch him without hurting him. He was terrified and angry at the same time. Riordan didn't think it was a good combination, so he watched Jim carefully.

"You hungry?" Jim nodded but looked like he was ready to bolt. "What do you think is going to happen when we get out of this car? You think we have a firing squad all lined up to take you out?"

"No," he said nastily, then looked at him again. "Do you? I don't blame you if you do. Like I said, I'm not a nice person. Haven't been for a long time either."

"You want to change that?" Riordan glanced at Storm when she asked. And when there was no reply forthcoming, she snapped her fingers at him and told him to look at her. "When I ask you a question, I demand an answer. I don't care if you think I'll like it or not, you little shit. You answer me honestly and without hesitation. Do you want to change?"

"Yes. But I don't think there's no hope for me." She asked him if he graduated from college. "I didn't even get to finish up regular school. Them teachers, they said I was too dumb to learn much and that I was wasting their time. So Dad popped me in the head again and took me out when I was fifteen."

"If your dad was here right now, I would…. We'll work on that too. You can get an education while you're working for Riordan." Storm looked at him, and he could see her sadness before she looked back at Jim. "We're here at our home, not at the jail or wherever you thought we were taking you. You can stay here until we get you squared away with a few things. But our house, our rules, understand?"

"Yes ma'am." Storm moved to the door and got out when it opened. Riordan stayed where he was and looked at Jim when he didn't move either. "I won't fuck this up. I mean, I'll try not to fuck this up."

"This is a rule you break and I will break you. You hurt my family—and that includes your sister—and you will never see me coming and your body will never be found." Jim stiffened and never took his eyes from his face. "Do you know what we are?"

"I heard rumors about you guys being something else. Nobody ever said for sure." Riordan told him they were tigers. "And you turn into them when you get mad, right? You just turn into this other thing?"

"We do, but we don't have to be mad to do it. Sometimes we just shift when we want to run and play in the woods." He put out his arm and let his cat take it. Claws formed. His fur covered the entire length of his arm in seconds. He supposed he could have just let himself be covered in fur and be done with it, but he wanted to make a point. "We're all cats but Andi, and I'm sure that'll change soon enough. Fuck with us, and I kid you not, you will die a horrible and painful death."

"Yes sir. I believe you." Jim looked at the open door, then back at him. "Why are you doing this for me? I know you don't like my family...well, except Andi I guess. But why are you doing this for me?"

"Because you're Andi's brother. And I have five of my own. Nobody is perfect, son. No one. And if you work with us and don't fuck up, you'll be a better man for it. You go on in the house now and we'll get you a meal that doesn't come out of the trash bin." Jim got out of the car then, and Riordan leaned his head back for a second hoping to Christ this wasn't a mistake.

When he entered his home, he went to his office. He knew that Jim was with Storm, but he needed to get a few things done before they had to leave again. Storm was working double duty nowadays. The president would call her up when he had a project for her to do, and she was working with Mac too. His business was doing well now, too, with the influx of new clients he'd taken on when they sort of moved into a different circle of people.

He'd had fifty-four emails since he'd left the house to go and rescue the aunts. Smiling, he thought of them calling here and telling them about young Jim in the back of the building.

"I think he's waiting on us to come out with the trash and leap on us. Maybe he'll want us to do things to him." He started to tell Lynn he doubted it when he heard Sally speak.

"What do you think he's going to be doing with us? We're as old as this building, and we're hiding in like a couple of relics. If that young man is that desperate, perhaps we should just let him lay out there. Because honey, if he wants us, he's going to be in for a big old disappointment." Sally huffed before continuing. "I swear to you, I'm going to make you stop reading those smut books. All you ever think about is sex."

"Maybe if you thought of it more, that nice man at the grocery store would give us a break on the meat." Riordan started to remind them that he was still on the line when Lynn spoke again. "And that other man, what's his name? Peter. That's it. Peter. You should flash him a little cleavage and we'd not have to pay those fines on the movies we had overdue last week."

"In order to flash anyone a little cleavage, I'd be lifting my shirt up from my hips. My bosoms have sagged that much in the last...are you still talking to someone on that contraption?" Lynn said it was him. "Oh for heaven's sake,

Lynn, we're more than likely scarred the man for life. He don't no more want to hear about our cleavage and sex life than I want him to know about it. Tell him to get on down here and rescue that boy."

"He don't care what I say. I think he's sweet on me." He was, on both of them. "You do love me, don't you, darling? You know that you're my favorite great nephew-in-law, don't you?"

"I also happen to be your only one, but yes, I love you both very much. And we'll be right down to see to him. Are you sure that it's young Jim?" She told him that she was as sure as rain. "Storm is here now, so we'll come down and get him. I'm betting he's hungry too."

"Oh, I don't doubt. Sister and I have been putting out a bag or two of leftovers for him. Well, they're not really left overs. I make him up a sandwich and put it in a Baggie for him. Then put it out when I see him." Riordan wondered how long they'd been doing that when she answered his unspoken question. "I don't think he's been doing it long. His daddy comes with him sometimes, and when he can't find things, he hits him. They come a mite early, but that man will beat him too much for not finding things. And when he does, he eats it all himself instead of giving any to that poor boy. It's why we do it for him. So he won't get beaten."

So, here he was with a man in his house that he knew nothing at all about. Who could, for all he knew, invite all kinds of riff raff inside and kill them all in their sleep. He looked at the door when Storm walked in and smiled at him.

"I was just thinking about Jim and what having him here can do." She didn't come any further in the room and he stood up. "What is it?"

"He's in the kitchen right now, talking to your mom and dad and sobbing like a little boy. I had to leave or show them that I have a heart. I can't let that get around, now can I? All she did was hug him for telling her she smelled nice." Riordan sat down, his knees weak with the relief that he wasn't going to have to kill someone. "I don't think that kid has been loved any more than Andi was. You think we can keep him?"

"He's not a pup." She grinned at him then. "I'm guessing from the look on your face that we have a son or something."

"We have a brother-in-law that needs us as much as Andi does, so yeah, I guess we do." She moved into the room. "The president just called. He wants us to go to China for him. And he said that if we want to stay an extra week, he'll pick up the tab."

"I love the way that man thinks. When do we leave? And what do we do about Jim?" She told him in the morning and nothing. He was going to stay with his parents. "Oh good. Just what the boy needs, my parents helping him out."

He knew that Jim would be fine now. He had no idea why, but he had a feeling that Jim was going to turn out all right.

CHAPTER 5

Andi didn't know what to do in the house, or with herself for that matter. There were so many rooms in it, most of them empty, that she was sure that she was going to need a map or something just to find her way around. Mac had left her about an hour ago, telling her that he'd be back before morning. He had to help Aedan with something.

"I can stay here. I'd like to." He nodded, but she was sure that he was torn. "I can take a nice bubble bath and then take a nap. I have to be at work in the morning at five, so this will be great."

"All right, but when I get home, I want you to be naked and in the bed waiting for me." He pulled her into his arms. "Are you sure? Aedan has a report to file for a client and his computer is fucking up. It's due tomorrow."

"Yes, go and help him. I'll be just fine here." After he left her, she had sat down on the floor and cried. Not that she expected him to stay with her. She knew at best this was going to be temporary, but the feeling of being overwhelmed took her breath away.

"Mrs.?" She looked at the man standing there, trying her best to remember his name when he smiled at her.

"Rogers, ma'am. I'm the new butler that Mrs. Harrison asked to come in and help out with the household."

"Yes. That's right. You're married to the cook, Bethany. She makes the best scones I've ever eaten." He nodded and flushed slightly. "What can I do for you?"

"There is a problem with…the kitchen, miss. It's…perhaps you should come and see for yourself. I know that this house is new to Mr. Mac, but I think we need to have some of the things repaired right away." She followed him and wondered aloud why he was asking her. "You're the new mistress of the house, we were told. Mr. Mac said that if we needed anything, you could help us."

"I don't know why he'd say that. I'm only hanging out here for…well, let's see what we can do about the kitchen first." She was worried that these people had the wrong idea about why she was here. Or perhaps they did know and were being polite about it. She was his sexual partner, nothing more. And Mac would have to explain that to them when he had time. Andi walked into the kitchen and nearly laughed. "I see. I guess we need to make a few phone calls."

She called the office, where she'd been told Mr. Mac was. There wasn't any answer that she needed, but a service did kick in and told her the office hours. Andi didn't know Mac's cell phone number, but Rogers had Storm's number. She didn't really want to call the other woman, but the sink was broken and they needed it worked on.

"Yeah, hi. It's Andi Collins. I work for you at the diner." Storm laughed and told her she knew who it was. "Okay, well, I have a problem here. The sink in the kitchen is broken. And I don't mean that the water is not working, but the whole sink is laying in the bottom of the shelf under it in pieces. Like someone with a sledge hammer beat it to shit. I can't get in touch with Mac to see what he wants to do."

"Did you try your link?" Andi asked her what that was. "Okay. I'm going to tell you how I was told to use it. Think of him. Just think of Mac and you should connect with him through your mind. He'll know it's you. It's sort of like a private number only the two of you can call. You can reach me too if we were to exchange blood. Which I think might be a good idea with you being a human and all."

"You make it sound like it's some sort of curse." Storm laughed and Andi felt her face heat up. "What will that help me with? I have this issue now."

"You'll see once you try it. If that doesn't work, I'm…. Hang on a sec." Andi wanted to try to reach out to Mac as Storm had suggested, but didn't want to be embarrassed again. She'd been doing that enough. "Okay, Ordan and another person are coming over to see if they can help. And so you're not thrown off by this, it's Jim, your brother."

"Why is he coming here? And where…did he hurt you? He can be mean, but mostly it's my father that makes him. I'm not saying I'm not afraid of him, but he can be nice when it suits him." She stopped talking when she heard Storm whistle. "I'm sorry."

"Don't be. But I wanted to tell you they were coming now before they got there. And Jim is staying here. He wants us to help him get out from under your dad and aunt. We had a long talk and he's going to go back to school and try to be an upstanding person." Andi asked her what if he didn't. "Then I kill him, bury him in the back yard, and we move on."

Andi wasn't sure if she was kidding or not. She really wasn't sure that she wanted to know either. Storm, according to Martha and Billy, had been in the army, something special. And could and would kill without much in the way of effort. Andi had a feeling that her brother would be dead long before he got to better himself. He was like their dad—too much to change like that, she thought.

"He's on his way over. Are you going to be all right with that? You have Rogers and his wife Bethany there, right? They can both protect you if he gets out of hand. They're both bears." Andi looked at the couple as they stood by the broken mess at the counter. Bears? She wondered what other kinds of shifters there were out there. "Andi, are you going to be all right with him being there?"

"Yes. I guess. He's not...bears? They're bears?" Storm laughed and she looked away from Bethany and Rogers, knowing that they must have heard her. "It's okay, I guess. I don't know what I'm going to say to him, but it's fine, I guess."

"Good. He's going to work on this, Andi, and when he does, you're going to be much easier around him. All of us will." Yeah, sure, and her father was going to be a priest too. "If you think you'll be all right, then I won't come over too."

"No, that's all right. I'm fine." She heard the car pull into the drive and looked out the back door. They must have been on their way or Mac lived closer to them than she'd thought. As they got out of the car, she told Storm that they were there and hung up. Turning to Rogers and Bethany, she told them what was going on.

"She told you about us, did she?" Andi nodded, suddenly a little afraid. "We'd never harm you. We owe Miss Storm everything, and you are her family. She saved our son for us when we all...she was in the service, you know? Well, our son was as well, but he'd been ordered to go there or he had to go to prison. When he was there, he met her. Not a good beginning to their relationship. I guess he insulted her. But Miss Storm, she got him on the right track and he did well for himself."

"I'm very glad for you. I think that's what she's trying to do with my brother. He's coming as well." She looked out the window again to see Mr. Harrison pulling things from the back of the truck and handing them to Jim. "I'm afraid of him…my brother, I mean. He's not always mean to me, but I don't know if my dad has sent him here to get me or not."

"He won't harm you. No one will so long as we can be here to help you." She nodded and asked if she could please go elsewhere while he was there. "Of course. Why don't you go to the living room and I'll bring you something to hold you over until dinner? I don't know what we'll be doing for dinner right now, but we can give you a nice snack."

Andi moved out of the kitchen and to the room that she felt the most comfortable in. It was also the only room with all of its furniture. Mac had told her that he'd only just moved in and was buying what he liked when he found it. She hoped that he found things like the furniture in this room for the rest of the house. She really liked this.

The house really was big. Five bedrooms and five baths on the upper floor. Four each on the second floor, as well a game room with a big screen that rolled from the ceiling, and seating like that of a movie theater. She had wondered if there might be popcorn, just kidding about it, when he showed her the big old fashioned popcorn maker in the corner of the room.

The main floor had the master suite with bathroom, a dining room that would hold fifty people she'd bet, kitchen, and living room. There were two bathrooms on this floor, not counting the one in the master bedroom, as well as a pantry that was as big as the place she stayed in before coming here. There was a linen closet, Rogers told her, as well as a plate room. There were no plates in it as yet, but he assured her that with the size of Mr. Mac's family, it would need to be filled up.

There was a pool and a pool house, also a gardener's shed, whatever that meant, as well as a butler's cottage and a garage. She'd yet to see either of those places, but was assured from Rogers that it was more than adequate for him and his wife. As she lay back on the big sofa, she wondered, not for the first time since coming here, what the fuck she was doing.

~~~

"I've been trying to reach my nephew. He's stupid, so I'm thinking that he's forgotten where his house is. There are times when I wish we'd just drown him like one of them stupid pups that end up at the house." Hester waited for the man behind the thick glass to answer her. She was sick to fucking death of getting the run around with these people. And having to come all the way down here to find Jim since that cunt of a niece wouldn't heel was really making her have to do things that she didn't think she should have. "Well? Is he there or should I call the morgue or something? Answer me, damn it."

She pounded her cane on the floor when he just stared at her. Hester had things to do and not one of them included hunting down Jim. Why George hadn't gotten rid of that kid when it was obvious to everyone that he was retarded was beyond her. Had she been living with him when that thing was born, he wouldn't have survived the night. Even that girl should have been taken out with the trash when she'd been born, and she might have had Jim not been lurking about like some fucking spy. Kids were the ruination of the world as far as Hester was concerned.

"Jim's not been around, Hester. Not for some time now. And had you called down here, I could have told you that over the phone." She didn't bother telling him that she didn't have a phone thanks to that ungrateful brat, Andi. "Would you like to go back and see your brother? We're moving him out in the morning."

"What do you mean, moving him out? You are not doing anything of the kind. What do you think is going to happen when you have to bring him right back? He should have been released days ago. I demand that you release him to me right now. This nonsense has gone on much too long for my tastes." He told her he wasn't doing any such thing. "You can be really brave on the other side of that glass, can't you? Well, let me tell you, you can't live back there. Yes, damn it all to fuck and back, take me to see George. You people are going to pay for this when I get me a lawyer."

He said something, but she couldn't understand him. Which was probably just as well. Hester hated the police. Hated everyone as a matter of fact, but if they had on a uniform or a suit, she'd just as soon shoot them between the eyes as to look at them. Fucking bastards, all of them.

When she was told to have a seat, she didn't. Standing her ground even though there were several people behind her made her feel like she was winning this war. And one thing that Hester liked to do was win. When the man behind her huffed at her, she turned and glared. The man backed up, just as he should have. Hester had showed him, she thought. Everyone was afraid of her. But then someone from behind him moved around her and to the front of the line and stood right in front of her to talk to the idiot behind the glass. Like she wasn't even standing there.

"What do you think you're doing? I'm being helped. You get your ass back in line and be quick about it." He didn't move, so she poked him in the ass with her cane. "I'm talking to you."

Before she could hit him this time, which was what she had planned, he turned and jerked her cane from her. Hester started to reach for it, to bash him over the head with it, when he just snapped it over his knee and dropped the pieces on the floor. As he turned back to the window and the fool behind it, she could see the officer laughing. Well fuck that shit, she thought.

Reaching for him this time, intent on slapping the shit right out of him, she had only brushed her fingers over his arm when he turned and grabbed her arm and pulled it up behind her in a quick move. No one had dared touch her for as long as she could hold a stick in her hand. But this man, this dead man—because he would be when she was finished—was shoving her towards the seats against the wall and then into one of them.

"You sit there and shut up or I will shut you up." She started to stand up when he leaned down to within an inch of her face. Hester Casey did not get treated this way. "You do not want to fuck with me, lady. I've had a really shitty day so far, and I need to do this for a friend of mine. So help me, I will fuck you up if you get out of that chair."

She might have gotten up. Hester was at the point where she was going to, too. But he snapped his teeth at her, his body taking on a thickness that reminded her of large cats that had been in the zoos when she'd been made to go to them. When he stood up, towering over her now that she was seated, she saw something run along his arms and neck, all the way to his face, that made her back from him and her belly lurch up.

He was a monster. One of those shifter things who could change into creatures and murder you in the night. Hester had heard of them, these things that were an abomination to the human race, and had been telling George and the rest of the idiots that was where the government money was going. Right to research on those things to make them. There was no way that anything like that had ever been born. They were making them so that they could take over the world.

When her name was called a few minutes later, the other man was gone, as was the line that had continued to move when he left. She was going to hunt him down too and show him a thing or two about Hester Casey. As she was being led back to see George, she thought of all the things she was going to say to him. Starting with him getting his ass home again.

"Hester. I didn't think you'd come to see me. It's been a long time since…I was wondering where you went to." She sat down on the chair that was in the room, pissed off again that no one had pulled it out for her. George was sitting across from her with cuffs on and an outfit that she disliked. Hester looked at the idiot in blue in the corner and wished she had her cane.

"Get these things off of him and find him another shirt to wear. This makes him look like a criminal and I will not have it." The officer that stood there only smiled at her. "Are you stupid? You heard me, remove them. He's got rights too."

"So does the woman he pulled a gun on. As well as the one he was dragging by her hair down the hallway. And I'm not going to take them off unless you think your visit is over." The man rocked back on his heels as he continued. "Or I could go get Liam for you and you can have another conversation with him. He was in a right foul mood when he left, thanks to you. Nicest man I ever met, and you managed to make him almost lose it."

"Me? I didn't do nothing. And if you're talking about that thing that roughhoused me, well, I plan to get his ass too." She looked at George when he asked her what was going on with this person. "You let me worry about this, and you work on getting out of here so I can get back to doing things the way I want. What the hell are you doing in here anyway? Pulling a gun on someone ain't a crime the last time I looked. Whoever she was, I'm pretty sure that she deserved it. Should have killed her if you ask me. Murdering somebody, we could have hid the body. And that daughter of yours too. She needs her ass kicked and chained up like I told you from the beginning."

"Hester, what woman are you talking about? I don't have a daughter." George looked confused and he laughed with the officer. "I don't think I want to talk to her any more. She's making my head hurt. Can you make her leave me alone?"

"I most certainly am not leaving you. What is wrong with you? Why are you acting so...like somebody drugged you up? Is that what they did? They brought you in here, drugged you up so you'd do what they told you? I'm telling you, George, the government is trying their best to kill off people like us. I'm talking about Andi. Your daughter that's an ungrateful bitch. And your son too. What is wrong with you?" George looked at her with this sort of glazed look, then his nose started to bleed. She was worried that he'd bleed out, and she reached for him to look into his eyes when the officer told her to put her hand back, no touching the prisoner. His body blocked her from her brother and that pissed her off more than she had been. Hester slapped the cop when he dared to get in her way.

Things happened almost too fast for her to realize that she should have not done that. At least when she didn't have her trusty cane. Her body was pressed against the wall now, her arm pulled up behind her back again, and she was being read some rights that didn't apply to her. She was exempt from shit like that. Hester Casey made her own fucking rules. When she struggled to get away, he pressed her harder against the wall and she was having a hard time breathing because of it.

"You're under arrest, Hester." She tried to ask him what for when he spoke again. "You can't slap me. I'm an officer of the law."

"I don't recognize you as the law. Let me go, you moron. I'm here to talk to my brother, not have you trying to get your jollies pretending to fuck my ass. What sort of drugs did you give him? Tell me now so I can have you shot." He laughed and Hester saw stars when he smacked her head against the unforgiving glass she was next to now. "I'm going to have your badge, you fucking prick. See if I don't."

As she was being led down the hall by not one but four officers, Hester told them all what she was going to do to them and that they had no rights over her. One of them told her to shut up, and she lunged at him and he laughed when she tripped up, falling on her ass right there in front of them.

"I'm an American citizen. And I got me rights." He told her that he did as well. "I don't give a flying good fuck about your rights. Bring me that dumbass niece of mine. I want her here now. I don't like her, but she's the only one besides me with even a lick of sense, and let me tell you, that ain't saying all that much. Get Andi Collins here now."

"Andi? I don't think you want to mess with her anymore, Hester. She's got her life in order, and you won't be fucking it up anymore. Not unless you have a death wish or something." The man that had attacked her first was laughing as he continued. "I don't think she'll come down here anyway. I think her and Mac are getting their house all set up."

"What do you mean, getting their house set up? I never gave her permission to do any such thing. If she has money to do shit like that, she's going to turn it over to me, not get her a house. Fucking whore. She'll pay the price of that if she thinks she can get things by me. Besides, she has a home. At my house. And when she gets there I'm going to show her what it means to be loyal to your family. She's left us without quite long enough. I want you to get her here." The man nodded but didn't move to do anything she was ordering him to do. "I swear to Christ, I've never met a more stupid bunch of fools in my entire life. Get. Andi. Here. Fucking. Now."

"I'll call her in the morning. Meantime, you are going to be put in that pretty little outfit like the one your brother has on and spend the night in a cell. You need anything?" Before she could tell him she needed him to let her go so she could knock the shit out of him, he had her picked up and shoved in the cell, and was walking away before she could form a thought.

"Get back here, you idiot. You hear me? I said to get back here. I'm going to hurt you when I get out." For the next twenty minutes she screamed at them. Finally, when she was so hoarse that she couldn't speak, she sat down on the edge of the bed. There was a bright orange jumper on the bed, but she refused to put it on. There wasn't a dressing room in here, and if they thought she was going to use that toilet hanging on the wall, well, she'd piss the bed before that happened. She just might anyway.

All night she was going to be stuck here if they didn't get that fucking niece of hers. Hester yelling at them had gotten her nowhere, and when one of them would come down the hall to, she supposed, count her, they would not say a single word to her, nor would they look in her direction only to see that she was still there. Hester was fuming when she saw the sun coming up from her little window in the fucking cell the next morning.

Just as the lights were coming on down the long hallway, she heard someone walking. The click-click of shoes on the hard surface had Hester waiting on her bed. Whoever it might be, they had better have the keys to this cell and a damned good lawyer. She was going to fucking sue them all. But when she looked up at the two people standing there, she was reminded of the man from earlier, the one that had knocked her around unnecessarily. It was not him, but he looked like him enough to know they were related.

"What the fuck do you want?" The woman looked familiar to her as well, but it was the man that she was talking to. Women were not smart enough, as far as Hester was concerned, to even bother with. She had always been the exception to the rule in being smarter even than all men she had ever encountered. "Are you getting me the fuck out of here? If not, then go the hell away."

"You had them call for me. What is it you want?" She looked at the woman and stood up. "Well? I'm sure you have a long list of things you think I'm going to do for you, but I'm not. Just so you know."

"I don't know you. Why are you even speaking to me? Go away." Hester moved closer to the bars and looked at her. The woman had her hair down, something that Hester did not approve of, as well as stylish clothing. A blue sweater that hung to her knees, jeans that looked too tight, and boots. Hooker boots she called them, the kind that went to the knee. "Who the hell are you?"

"It's me. Andi Collins. Your niece. They told me that you wanted to see me. So what is it? I didn't really want to come down here, but I thought I'd see what it was you wanted." Hester wanted to deny it was her, but knew that this creature before her was just who she said. "Well? What do you want?"

"You will not speak to me that way, young lady. I am your elder and I demand respect from you. Where is that idiot of a brother of yours, too? I'm going to start laying down the law again, and the two of you are going to suffer greatly for this...whatever you call what you've been up to." Hester looked her up and down. "And you'll not be wearing whore clothing like that either. I'm guessing that's what he is to you? Some sort of good fuck that buys you things? You're finished with that as well. Get rid of him and get me out of here."

"This is the man I'm living with, Cormac Harrison. Mac, this is my Aunt Hester, my father's sister. She's a nasty woman." Hester started to speak but was cut off by Andi. She saw stars, she was so pissed now. "We came down here to see what you wanted. As for the way I'm dressed? I love this. And I plan on wearing more pretty things. They make me feel good about myself. Something you never did."

"You think you can talk to me that way because there are bars between us? When I get you home, you're going to pay for this. Get me out of here so I can teach you a lesson like I used to when you were a baby." Andi simply told her no. "No? No? You do as I say, Andi, or so help me I'll make you regret it. You will anyway, but I'm not going to be treated this way. And where is that simpleton brother of yours? Don't think I didn't notice that you didn't answer that either. I've been looking for him for several days now, and when I find him, he's going to regret it. Then that fucking bastard of a cop decided to toss me around like nothing, and now they think they can hold me in here. Get me out of here, Andi. Right now."

"No. And if there is nothing else you want, I'm going home now." Hester watched her as she backed from the cell. "You're a horrible, mean woman, and I'm glad that Jim and I managed to figure that out before you killed us. Jim is safe from you, by the way. You and Father can go straight to hell for all I care."

Hester screamed at her to come back here, but she only moved out of the area.

CHAPTER 6

Mac wasn't sure who was more upset, he or Andi, as he drove them to the shopping center. He was sure that she would rather be doing anything else but picking out furniture, but she'd told him that it was fine. Mac reached for his mom again.

She's going to be all right, son. I just know it. This is the best thing for her, to tell her relatives what she thinks of them. And I'm sure it took a great deal out of her to stand up to that woman like you said. He told her that it broke his heart to see her this upset. *Well of course it does. When you love someone, that's what happens.*

He started to tell him mom that he didn't love her, but he glanced over at Andi and realized in the moment that he did. Christ, he loved her. When his mom started talking again, he had to have her stop so he could breathe around this new information. Mac was in love.

I've never been in love before. He felt her laughter and wanted to find her and hug her for telling him what his heart already knew. *Do you suppose she loves me too?*

I would think she does. You're a good boy...man, I suppose. And if she hasn't realized it as yet either, it'll come to her when you tell her how you feel. She laughed again. *Your father said to tell you to change her and get her fat with his grandson.*

I'd like that as well.

As soon as they parked, Mac pulled her into his arms. He'd driven over to the market district, knowing that whatever they bought, some of it they'd be able to put in the back of his brother's truck. Andi didn't say anything, but she did rest her head on his shoulder.

"Will you marry me?" He hadn't meant to say that or to even ask at this moment. But now that the words were out there, he decided that was just what he wanted. When Andi looked up at him, he kissed her on the mouth as he continued. "I know that you think this is really fast. And I guess for most it would be. But for us, our kind—tigers, I mean—we fall in love quickly and love hard. And I do…love you, I mean. And making you my wife is what I want more than anything in this world. Dad said I should get you fat with him a grandchild, and I think that's—"

She put her hand over his mouth and he realized he was babbling. Mac kissed the palm of her hand and pulled it away before kissing her again, this time with all the love he felt for her.

"You're very…why?" He asked her what she meant. "Why do you think you want to marry me? And I'm not saying no, but just to have a kid is not a good enough reason."

"No, it's not. I would find that to be a perk." She growled low and he laughed. "Also, if you would like, I'd very much like to convert you to what we are. A tiger. That way we can go running in the woods together. Have—"

Mac stopped talking when she growled again. He tried to think how best to answer her. Because he had a feeling that this was going to be the most important answer he could ever give a person in his life.

"Why do I want to marry you? I suppose I could tell you the story about how, as a cat, falling in love is quick and with the only person that I will ever love. I could tell you that tiger shifters mate for life and that marriage is a way for you to be legally mine, even though in my heart you are already mine. But I don't want you to think those are the only reasons why I want to marry you." He felt something wash over him and knew that it was a great calmness, and that his cat was helping him. "I'm in love with you. And I think I have been since the first time I saw you. I would love to grow old with you, have children with you, and grandchildren later on. But the real reason that I want to marry you is that I want to commit to you. Show you that no matter what, I belong to you and only you. That whatever I have is yours, whatever you have is ours. I want nothing more than to know every day when I wake that you're there, and when I go to bed at night, it is with you in my arms."

He watched her face and wondered if he'd gone too far. Or perhaps not far enough. As she sat there, he wondered what was going on in her mind and heart. Mac was tempted to look but only held her. Then she looked out the front window of the truck.

"No one, not in my entire life, has said that they loved me. My mother might have, but she died when I was very young so I have no idea if she did or not. My father hated me, and told me that on numerous occasions. Aunt Hester...well, you've met her, so you know what she feels about me, or just about anyone, I guess. Jim never...I think Jim might not know what love is either. And there were times when we were growing up that I thought that he perhaps felt something for me." Mac held her to him, knowing that everything she said was true. He'd talked to

Jim the other day, and knew that neither of them had had a good childhood, or much of an adulthood either. When she turned back to him, he held his breath, afraid of her next words. "I don't know what I feel for you, Mac. It might be love. I know that I've never felt this way before with anyone. I like the way you treat me. I know there are times when you get frustrated with me because I'm so afraid, but I think with you I can move on from that too."

"I love you." She nodded and laid her head over his heart. "It only beats for you, my heart. I'm here with you because I don't want to be with anyone else."

"I see your mom and dad." He turned and looked and saw them too. "I think...would you give me a little time to think about this? I don't...I like being with you, but I need to think."

"You take as long as you want. But don't be surprised if I tell you every minute that I love you with all my heart." She grinned at him. "Okay...shopping, dinner, then back to our place for a night of making love."

As he walked up to his parents, Mac felt lighter than he had in years. Holding Andi's hand, he wanted to shout to the world that he had found her. His one and only true love. Feeling a little sappy, he kissed his mom and hugged his dad. Entering the shopping center, buying furniture that the two of them were going to use for the first time, had him giddy.

You're a sap. He felt his brother's touch and told him to fuck off. *Yeah, I got my own mate for that, thanks. Anyway, I wanted to tell you that Storm has Jim assigned to this guy she knows that's going to whip him into shape. I'm not sure what that means, but I don't think he's going to be the same afterwards.*

You mean with his education? Riordan told him it was everything. *I see. And you're telling me because you want me to tell Andi?*

Yeah. As timid as she is, Storm said that she's going to pop one of these days soon, and she wants to be there to see it. She seems to think that your mate is going to be epic when she lets that tightly held temper go. Mac said he didn't think she had a temper like that. *Oh, you need to talk to Storm about that. She said she knew this guy once that was being beat to shit about something. She didn't tell me what so I just assumed we didn't want to know. But anyway, when he finally had had enough, the guy took out seven men with his bare hands. She said it was a sight she'd never forget.*

They were currently in the bedroom department of the center and he wandered off, trying to find a place where he could talk to his brother without being interrupted. Mac was sure that Storm was wrong about Andi. The woman had had people pounding on her for years and had never snapped. He also wanted to tell him that he'd asked Andi to marry him.

I told her I loved her and she needs to think about it. I want her to tell me now, but I'm not going to rush her. Riordan told him that was a good plan. *She said that no one has ever loved her before, or even said it to her. Jim either.*

That's probably right. And it would explain a great deal. How did the visit with her aunt go? I'm assuming that didn't pan out like the woman wanted either. He told him no. *I was talking to Tyler earlier, by the way, and he said that she'd be released today with a fine and court date. You might want to tell Andi so she can keep an eye out for her.*

He told him he would as he watched Andi bounce on one of the beds with his mom nearby. Mac felt his cock ache to join her, show her the proper way to bounce on a bed. Embarrassed just a little, he asked his brother what had been on his mind since getting out of the shower with Andi this morning.

Do you ever get tired of Storm? I mean, not being around her, but…Christ, I don't know. Does the sex part ever slow? Do you continue to want to fuck her every time you see her?

Riordan laughed and Mac wanted to tell him to forget it.

Yes. And I'll tell you something, she's no different. I mean…well, no details, but if we come up missing, don't go looking for us and I'll do the same for you. Mac leaned against the wall and smiled. *Go buy some shit for your house and stop bothering me. I have a mate I want to nail.*

The rest of the afternoon was spent looking at everything under the roof. When dinner time rolled around, they ended up at his parents' favorite restaurant, a Mexican place that served the best tamales he'd ever eaten. And then they went home. Mac thought perhaps it was the most fun he'd had in a long time shopping.

And as soon as he was in the house, Mac pulled Andi into his arms and showed her with his entire body how much he loved and wanted her. When he lifted his head and looked down at her, he fell in love with her all over.

~~~

Andi wanted to go to the bedroom, but the more Mac touched her, unbuttoning her clothing so that he could, the less and less appeal it had to her to let go of him. And when he took her bare breast into his mouth and sucked hard, she held him there and tried to think if anyone was in the house right now.

"I want to take you outside and run with you." Before she could tell him yes, because that sounded good to her, he smiled. "Go in the yard by the tree line and take off all of your clothing but these boots. I want to fuck you against a tree with you wearing them."

"What if someone sees us?" He told her that they were their woods and if they did come on his property, they should get a show. "Are you going to be your tiger when you chase me?"

"Yes. He's going to run you down and then eat you. Fucking you with his tongue too." Her body heated and she knew that he could smell her when his nostrils flared. "Go. Before I change my mind and take you right here."

She went out to the yard and away from the two houses on the back side of the property. Andi was excited, but she was also afraid. Being naked in the house was one thing, but out in the open was something entirely different. As she laid her clothing out, she thought about what Mac might be about to do to her.

His cat was sexy. So was Mac. The two of them, different but alike in many ways, made her come so hard when they touched her. And also they both made her feel like she was everything to them. Sitting down on a log, she pulled off her boots to take her pants off and felt her pussy warm at the thought of being dressed this way, naked, with only her boots to keep her from stepping on something hard. When she was finished zipping the boots back up, she saw him coming toward her.

Had anyone told her that she'd be willing to have a big Bengal tiger coming toward her, much less touch her, she would have said they were insane. But now, all she could think about was her cat. The way he touched her, his fur warming her skin. When he stopped moving and sat down, she reached out to him like Storm told her to do and felt the connection.

I've never done this before, as you know. Do I just run? He told her yes and to hide too. *You'll find me, right? I won't be lost out here.*

No. I'll find you. Right now I can smell your pussy, heated and ready for us. She ran her fingers through the wet curls, and he growled at her. *Go. He wants to mark you too when he's eaten his fill of you.*

Andi took off running. It was a little disconcerting at first, being naked with only a pair of boots on. But when he ran her down, knocking her to the soft grass the first time, he licked her pussy from gate to clit, then told her to go again, but to try harder to hide.

The trees were dense on this part of the land, but she knew that hiding behind them would get her found quickly again. Not that it didn't hold a great deal of appeal, for him to lick her that way again, but she knew this was going to be fun for them both. As she found a hollow log, she moved deep inside of it and waited for him to come for her.

He touched his tongue to her leg, just above the boots she had on. Screaming at the startling feeling, he pulled her from her hiding place with his great mouth on her boot. Mac told her to spread her legs and he did it again, this time bringing her so close that she wanted to beg him for more.

Go. And remember, everything you touch, you leave your scent on. Not that I couldn't find you anyway, but that will keep me from finding you so quickly. She got up, her body shaking with need, and took off again. This time she was careful not to let branches touch her so much. She didn't reach out to trees when she walked by them afraid of falling on her ass. And when she came to a cropping of large stones, she moved between them.

She could hear the birds when they stopped making sounds and knew that he was close. Andi heard branches breaking close by too, and wondered if he was right next to her. Being as still as she could, controlling her breathing, she closed her eyes and waited for him to find her. Needed for him to find her.

The wait was killing her. And she was sure that he was right there, waiting for her to make a small sound so he could pounce. When she couldn't stand it any longer, she moved so she could look out and screamed again when he was sitting there waiting.

Come here. We've had enough play. Andi moved out of the rocks and started toward him. *No, lean back on the stone there. He wants to eat you while you stand there.*

Lying back against the biggest stone, Andi felt sexy, her body beautiful. And when the cat's big head moved between her legs, she opened her thighs for him and cried out when he licked his thick tongue over her clit.

He fucked her with his tongue, the texture of it bringing her twice before he told her to lie down. As soon as she was down on her back, her knees bent and her pussy open for him, her big cat moved over her, his mouth and tongue doing things to her that he'd not been able to do while she'd been standing.

Come for us. Come and fill us. She let go of the scream she was holding. It felt like it was the string that her climax had been held to. As soon as she cried out that she was coming, she felt her body release. It was magnificent, the way her body tumbled over and over into a pleasurable abyss. Every time she came, every release she had, he told her to come again. To fill their needs too. And when the cat licked her thigh, she knew that he was going to bite her hard and that it would be a marking.

His teeth seemed to tear into her. Andi tried to be brave, not scream, but when he jerked at her flesh, his mouth tearing at her instead of just biting, she screamed again and again until she knew that Mac was with her. His body seemed to be protecting hers when he was over her.

"You're ours." She nodded, knowing in that moment she was in love with Mac. "I need you, baby. Are you still in pain?"

"No. Please, take me, mark me as he did." He filled her, his cock not just entering her but seeming to become a part of her. And when he began moving, his big body slamming into hers, Andi wrapped her legs and arms around him to hold on. "I love you, Mac. I love you so much."

He didn't slow but seemed to be faster, his cock thicker. And when he licked her throat, right where she knew her pulse was pounding, he sank his teeth into her and she did the same to his shoulder, tasting blood as it filled her mouth.

Sucking on the wound, filling her mouth over and over with his essence, she knew that he was loving it. When he came twice more, cum filling her as he had her heart, Andi licked along the wound at his shoulder and for some reason wasn't surprised when it sealed. This time when she came, darkness swallowed her and Andi thought if she were to die right now, she'd be happy and content.

When she opened her eyes, Mac tightened his hold on her when she started to move. At his nod, she looked in that direction and saw the family of deer having their dinner. It was the most beautiful thing she'd ever seen.

The buck was watching. Not them but everywhere. He'd look around, nibble on grass then look around, maybe not knowing that there was a cat nearby, but not taking any chances that his family would be harmed. Always on alert for his family. The fawn and her mother were having dinner at their leisure. Nothing seemed to disturb them, but Andi had a feeling that she was just as on guard as her mate.

They've been coming out at night since I've moved in. When winter comes, we'll put out something for them so they can survive. Sadly, the deer population around this area has been about wiped out with hunters. Andi asked Mac if he planned to let more come in. *Yes. Right now there are three families here. Also a wolf pack that are not shifters. A bear and her cub too, but I've not seen much of them. On Riordan's property there are several families of deer, but he doesn't hunt them either.*

Storm told me that Rogers and Bethany were bears. Will they run with the two that live here too? He told her no. Bears were not a social group, and shifters and bears didn't seem to get along as well as shifter bears did. *Should I not go out here alone?*

There are all kinds of shifters on all of our lands. Most of them are friends with Storm, and she lets them roam their land because they keep an eye on things. Same here too. If you see someone on the land, I don't want you to assume that they're friendly, but don't shoot them either.

The deer took off at some sound that they heard. Mac rolled her to her back and looked down at her. "Did you mean it when you said that you loved me?"

"Yes. I love you. I didn't know, but I do now." He kissed her, his cock at her thigh stirring enough to have her turning toward him. "Make love to me, Mac. Right here."

He watched her face and thought that another man could not love a woman as much as he did her. When he was between her legs, his cock thick at her entrance, he told her he loved her as he entered her slowly. It felt wonderful, this way he was making love to her.

Each stroke of his cock brought her closer to him. Each time he touched his mouth to her body, she felt heated by it. His fingers on her skin seemed to brand her, in a way that made her feel loved and cherished.

"I love you, Andi. With all that I am." She nodded, too overwhelmed by everything to speak. "Marry me. Make me the happiest man in the world."

Her climax took her. All of her. Not just her body but her heart and soul too. And she knew that it belonged to one person. The man filling her again. Screaming out, she told him yes. Yes. Yes, as she fell into a darkness that welcomed her like a babe to a mother's bosom.

Waking once, she realized that she'd been carried home at some point. Her body was held by Mac, the room awash in darkness. When he spoke to her, his voice soft and sexy, she smiled at him.

"You said yes, by the way. Several times, as a matter of fact." Turning in his arms, she looked at him, seeing his eyes shining in the moonlight. "I'm going to hold you to that. And in the morning we'll go and apply for a license. All right?"

"Yes. I think that's a great idea." Rolling so that her back was to him, his chest felt warm against her backside. "Then when we get home you can convert me. I've decided that I want to be able to mark you like you did me."

"We should wait a few days, at least until we get your aunt squared away. You'll be out for several days, and I don't want her coming here and trying to hurt you." She turned back to him again. "She's making trouble for you and Jim. Riordan told me when we got back to the house. Jim is going away for a few months, so we're not worried about him, but you…we want you to stay with one of us at all times."

"What is it she's doing?" He asked her if he could tell her in the morning, and that way they'd be fresher. "Is it bad, Mac? Is anyone in your family going to be hurt by her too? I can go away."

"No, you won't. And so you know, you're as much family to them as I am. My family has this. We'll make sure you're not hurt." Nodding, she rolled to her side again, thinking of all the things her aunt could do to her now that she'd found happiness. "I love you, Andi. We're going to be just fine."

She hoped so. Finding love was the greatest thing that had ever happened to her. She didn't want to lose it so soon after getting it. When Mac wrapped his arms around her, she closed her eyes. She just hoped that her dad stayed out of this too.

CHAPTER 7

Mason had been going to see George Collins every day for a week now. He was pleased with the results of his mind control. Working with Browning again had been a blast, and he hoped that he'd be able to continue to do things much like this for her. He even liked her mate. Riordan was a good man. When his name was said, he had a feeling that he'd been called to a couple of times and grinned at Mac.

Mac was...he liked him a great deal. There was something about him that let you think that he was too calm and cool to ever get upset. But he was pretty sure, much like his mate, that he had a temper just below that charming show of teeth that would hurt whoever unleashed it.

"I asked if you're sure about this thing. That he's not going to bother us again." Mason nodded and looked over at Andi. She did not deserve what had been happening to her since birth. "She's afraid of him."

"And with good reason." He said her name, and she looked at him finally. "Are you afraid of me too?"

"No. I have no idea why, but I'm not. I would be afraid if we weren't on the same side. I think, and this is just me,

but I think you're one scary vampire when you need to be."
He assured her that he was. "And this thing you did to my
dad, it won't...I don't know, it won't go away?"

"Not in his lifetime. When he thinks of you, he'll get a
pain in his head. Which, I must confess, is not nearly as
much pain as I would like for him to have. Then if he
continues to think of you in any way, or even your brother
now, then he will get sick with his head pains. It will
become so bad if he persists that he will have a brain
hemorrhage and die. I do not want him coming to you with
ill intent again. And he will not."

When Andi nodded, Mason looked at Storm Browning.
He supposed her name was no longer Browning really, but
Harrison. But she'd been the first of the two names long
enough that it had stuck. She was the only reason he was
alive now, and not ash beneath the shoes of mankind.

"Andi, he's tried to do the same to your aunt, but
she's...well, evil I guess. More so than your father." Andi
snorted at Browning, and Mason smiled. He would bet
anything these people did not know half of what this girl
had lived with, even in the last five years. He figured that
she needed to tell them, if not for them to be aware but so
that she could get it out of her heart and mind.

"You should tell them everything." Andi looked at him,
and he could see her fear. "They will not judge you, though
I have no idea why they would even think anything badly
toward you. But they should know everything your aunt is
capable of. I know some, but not all. Some things...some of
them I would bet not even her brother knows about her."

"I don't know what you're talking about." He said
nothing but watched her. When she got up to pace, he
looked over at Mac and could see that the man was
completely in love with his mate. Good, things would go

much better if they were in love. "She's evil, you know that."

"I do. But they don't, not really. They can think it, but you know for a certainty that she is, don't you? I've seen things in her mind that frighten even me. Knowing that this monster has been allowed to roam the earth makes me want to go out and drain her. I won't; her blood, I'm sure, would be nasty and bitter." Andi nodded and he had to smile. "Tell them, Andi. Tell them what she did to you the week before you left home all those years ago. The reason you left home."

He wasn't sure she was going to answer him. Or to tell them what he'd found out. When she'd called Hester a monster, Mason thought that any monsters alive would have been insulted to have been put in the same category as her. Lynn and Sally entered the room and all the men stood up.

These two women had been entertaining him for days now. With their permission, he'd been resting during the day in their old home's sublevels. The house was in need of some very big repairs. And he'd been having some work done on it while he was there, in payment for them letting him stay. Lynn winked at him when she handed him a rose from her garden.

"I have no idea why I thought of you when I saw that." He looked at the rose and knew the origin of the rose and even the breeder. "I just love roses, and I'd completely forgotten that there was a garden here until Riordan hired a gardener. Do you know what it is?"

"I do, actually. It's called Madam de Watteville. It was first bred by Jean-Baptiste André and discovered by a woman by the name of Margaret Furness a few years later. She found it in a garden that started around nineteen hundred near Mildura on the Murray River in Australia." He looked up, thinking he'd given too much information about a rose, when Sally asked him what the name of the family home was and had he visited. "The home was called Kombacy, and yes, but a gentleman never tells when or why he visited."

They laughed, as did he. When he put the pretty little pink and white tea rose in his lapel, he noticed that Andi was still at the window she'd paused at. He wondered if she had any idea how beautiful she looked there.

"I'd been ready to move out for weeks. But every time I did, something would happen. Mostly it was my money that would come up missing, or...or I'd have to heal. I was forever—" Andi looked at him as she continued. "I guess you know that I didn't fall all those times. That I was beaten, sometimes so badly that I would end up in the clinic. Never the hospital. They asked too many questions. And I would lie. I think they knew what was going on, don't you?"

"I'm sure of it. But they, like you, were terrified of Hester. She had made everyone's life a living hell with the information that she would hold over them." She nodded and he told her to go on. "They have to understand her."

"The week before I was moving out, I had taken all my money and put it in the bank. I was nineteen then, and someone had told me that I could open an account without their permission, nor did I need them to sign for me. All that time before, I'd been told by them, my father and aunt, that I had to be twenty-five. That without their co-signature that I would never be able to have an account. I never checked on it because if they were right, and I did have an account, it would have done me as little good to have it as it was for me to keep hiding it at home. So when I got the account, the first thing I did was open me a post office box as well. Nothing that I had was going to be going home again." Mac got up and went to her, holding her in his arms as she continued. "I had packed up what little I had — there really wasn't that much — and had taken it out of the house a little at a time. I worked for a diner then, and he'd been nice enough to let me stash things there until I got ready to move in."

Mason could feel the sorrow in the room. They loved her as well. And Mason would bet that if Hester came here now, any one of them would lay down their life for her. And then Browning would break her neck and bury her in the back yard without missing a beat.

"Go on, my dear. Tell us what happened when you got ready to leave home." Bri took her husband's hand into hers and held him. The two of them, the Harrison elders, were the nicest people Mason knew. And that was saying a lot. "You tell us so that when the witch comes here we can all kick her bottom."

"Ass. Under the circumstances, let's call it what it is. We'll kick her ass." Browning winked at Ordan — Riordan's father — and then looked at Andi again. "You tell me what she did to you and I'll make a few calls and that will be the end of her. I am not without contacts."

"I don't want you to kill her. I want her to suffer, but I want her to suffer for the rest of her life." That was what he'd been hoping for. The woman to take a stand. "She beat me with that cane of hers. Beat me so badly that I had to have ninety-four stitches in my back and some in my legs. She hit me in the head, on the legs, and belly. I don't even know when she stopped because at some point, I lost consciousness. On top of a concussion and a torn up ankle, I was black and blue from the beating too. But I left, hobbled out of that bed and to the front of the house, where I flagged down a perfect stranger to take me to the hospital. And when I got there, I called the police."

"And they couldn't do anything about it, could they?" Andi shook her head at Sally. "Of course not. If you had beaten her, the police would have been all over that. I'm betting that she has this little black book that she keeps notes on about people. We saw that once, didn't we, Lynn? Watching one of those police drama things, remember that?"

"You're going to have to narrow it down a little more than that. You have every cop show and drama recording every time one comes on. I swear to you, Sally, you could be a detective with all the information you get from those things." Stormy told her that they were usually wrong about some of the stuff. "Oh, what do you know, Stormy, dear? Your idea of dealing with someone is to pull out your gun and shoot them. I'd like a little conversation before I just snap their necks like a twig."

The room was silent. Mason was sure that even Lynn was surprised by her comment. But then Andi laughed, hard. Then Ordan and his wife. Soon the entire room was laughing, and Mason thought it was the best medicine for what was going on.

~~~

Mac wasn't sure what he was supposed to say to Jim, but he'd come to see him when he asked. Ennis was with him. They were going to go pick up a few things on the way back home for dinner for Andi, as she was cooking for them all. Then they were going to help them rearrange furniture that had been delivered before he'd left.

Jim came out of the room he'd been waiting in and stood there looking like a lost child. Mac watched him, dressed in clean clothing and a jacket that looked brand new. He had sent someone shopping for him when he'd been notified that he was without certain basic items. Even a toothbrush wasn't in his things. Jim looked much younger than Mac thought he actually was.

He was too. His IQ was that of a nine or ten-year-old boy, the doctors said. But he had the ability to work at a single task better than most adults could. They had a name for it, but for the life of him, Mac didn't remember what it was. When Jim sat down, playing with his zipper on his new jacket instead of looking at him, Mac wondered what he was supposed to do now. Ennis told him to go carefully, the man had been though a great deal in the last few weeks. So when he started talking, Mac wanted to tell him to slow down, but he did before he could say anything.

"They're giving me a job where I can make my own money. And I don't have to share it with anyone but keep it for my own stuff. I have a place to stay too, but I have to have someone living with me so I don't forget to do things on my own. At least until I can prove to them that I won't go out and get myself tangled up in the wrong kind of people anymore. I can't drive no more either. I don't do so well with that, and they took away my license. But Stormy, she told me if I wanted to bitch about it too much I could go and live with Hester and she could cart my ass around if I wanted her to. I don't think she'd want to even if I did. I really like Stormy. She's nice and mean too. But she said she won't lie to me, and if I be good, she won't kill me either. I sure hope I don't make her want to kill me." Jim finally looked up at him. "I want you to tell my sister something for me, please."

"You should tell her." Jim shook his head and said he wasn't ready for that yet. "Why not? I'm sure she'd like to hear from you."

"No, she won't. Not yet anyway, the doctor told me. I have to see him every now and again so I can work on myself. And I don't know what to say to her yet. I'm not...I need to get me together where I can be a better brother to her. I've not been so far." Mac said nothing but noticed that Ennis had left the room. "They're going to send me to this school where I can learn a trade. The doctor said I should have been worked with when I was younger and I might have been a better adult. He blames my dad and aunt for that."

"Do you?" Jim looked at his zipper again but didn't answer. "How old are you, Jim? I know that you're older than Andi, but I don't think anyone ever said."

"I'm thirty-one. But my mom hurt me.... No, I'm not to say that any more either. It's not true. There was an accident at birth and I had the cord thingy wrapped around my neck and the doctors couldn't fix it. It wasn't her fault like Dad told me. And Aunt Hester told me that it was my fault too, but I know that it wasn't now. It weren't neither of our faults, just something that happens. But they did me wrong by not helping me." He looked up from the zipper. "I have new clothes, thanks to you. When I lived with my dad, he would make me steal things to get new. And sometimes he'd take me to the place where people would donate bags of things for people like us. Poor. But I don't think we were poor, were we, Mac?"

"Not from what I've been able to find out, no you weren't." There had been an insurance policy when their mom died. George hadn't been able to cash it in, no matter how many times he'd tried, when the kids were younger.

But he'd been able to live off a settlement from it. But when Jim and then Andi had turned twenty-one, that had stopped too. The benefactors were her children. And when they turned twenty-one, they were to get the money and no one else. But no one had bothered to cash it in. And after talking to Andi, he was pretty sure that no one had even told either of them about it. So the money had been sitting waiting for someone to take care of it since. "Money has been put into an account for you for your care while you're here, and then when you go away for a while. When you need things, you're to call me or Andi and we can have it taken care of. There is more than enough money for you to get just about anything you need."

"But you bought me these things, didn't you?" He told him that he and Andi had. "She doesn't like me. I don't blame her, but she doesn't. Dad…he made me be mean to her or he'd take my food from me. Most of the time he'd just beat me. It was hard to not do those things to her when he'd hurt me like he did. But she always made sure that I had something to eat when she could. I love her very much, you know."

He played with the zipper again, and Mac wondered what it was about it that seemed so fascinating. Then Jim started talking, mostly to himself, Mac thought. But it was no less chilling to him.

"I used to watch over her when she came home from the hospital after Mom died. Aunt Hester came to live with us when Mom was in the hospital, and then stayed when Mom passed away. Aunt Hester hated Andi more than she did my mom. But Aunt Hester would come into her room and try to smother her with the pillow or put her hand over her mouth and nose and try to kill her off. I caught her doing that a couple of times, so I moved into her room with her." The zipper went up and down faster now, like he was afraid of the words that were spilling from his mouth. "Then one night I didn't hear her. Andi, I mean…I didn't hear her breathing. Aunt Hester, she had come in when I was sleeping and took her out of her bed. When I went to look for her, Aunt Hester was holding her under the water in the tub. She was trying to kill my little sister."

"What did you do?" Mac was sure that whatever he'd done, it had made an enemy of his aunt for him. And when he stopped with the zipper and looked at him, Mac saw sorrow. And pain. "Did she beat you?"

"Told me I had no right to hit her like I did. I broke the broom on her, I was so scared that she was gonna kill little Andi. Then she just let go of her and I had to hit Aunt Hester again and again until she didn't move no more. I scooped up Andi and took her away from there." Jim sobbed now, much like Mac would bet he had all those years ago. "She near drowned her. And for what? There was no call for her doing that to my sister. None at all."

Mac got up and went to the couch where Jim was sitting and pulled the man into his arms. The zipper was still being pulled, but Jim leaned into him. When he started to cry, heart wrenching sobs that hurt his soul, Mac held him until he calmed down.

"I'd be appreciative if you would tell my sister something for me." The crying was finished now, so Mac moved back to his chair. Ennis had come in and left again, leaving the two of them alone for now. "She don't have to do nothing about it, but I want you to please tell her for me. Tell her that I'm sure sorry."

"About what?" Jim said that he'd not been a good brother. Hell, he'd not even been a good man. "I'll tell her. But you want her to believe you, then you work hard at this job you're going to get to do, save up your money, and make something of yourself. All right?"

"I can do that. I'm going to try my best to do that." When he was ready to go, Jim just got up and left. Mac sat there, his mind trying hard to grasp why someone would want to harm a child, a baby really. Ennis came back and looked upset, but didn't comment on Jim. They were in the car on the way home when everything Jim told him hit him.

"Pull over. Now. I'm going to be sick." Ennis pulled over, and Mac fell out of the truck. He landed on his hands and knees and stayed that way while he threw up twice. There wasn't much on his belly, thankfully, but he still felt like shit. Rolling to his ass, he looked up at his brother as he stood over him after handing him a bottle of water. "She tried to kill her. Hester tried to drown Andi when she was nothing more than a baby."

"That isn't even all of it." Mac asked him if he wanted to know. "Yes. I talked to Jim's doctor. When I got him in here, one of the conditions was that he had to see someone. Just to figure out what sort of person we were going to be dealing with. Now he's seeing him daily to help him work out...Christ, Mac, it's far worse than you can imagine. Hester let their mother die."

"I thought she died from childbirth." Ennis shook his head and sat in the dirt with him. "We can't kill her, can we? Hester, I mean. We can't just let Stormy hire some man she knows to go and find this bitch and make all of our lives a good deal better."

"Not legally. No. But when Andi and her mom came home from the hospital, Jim and his aunt were taking care of her. Catering to her, Jim told my friend, is what his aunt had called it. And Hester apparently thought that she'd had enough taking care of a brat, as she called Andi, and a lazy woman. So when April, that was her name, needed to get up to use the bathroom, Hester told her she was on her own, that she was done helping her. Jim tried to help her, but she was too weak and he wasn't strong enough to get her to the bathroom and back on his own. When his mom fell to the floor and started hemorrhaging, he panicked, and in doing so pissed off Hester so much that she beat him again. Then she made him hold his mother's body in his arms until she was dead. She bled out while Jim cried for Hester to please help him. And when his dad got home, he tried to tell him what had happened and George, in his infinite wisdom, cuffed the boy in the head and told him to clean up the mess. Can you imagine doing that? A little boy who just held his mother taking her last breath having to clean up the blood? Those people deserve whatever happens to them."

"Does Andi know?" Ennis said he didn't know. Jim had gone catatonic after that for a few hours, the doc had told him. "We have to do something about this woman. She has to pay for this."

"Yes, I agree. But as far as the law is concerned, she's done nothing wrong. I mean that they can prove. Yes, she hit an officer. Even Liam had a run in with her, but legally, she's clean." He'd bet that Storm could find something on her and said that to Ennis. "She'll kill her. You know that, right? Storm would just pull her gun, pop a bullet in her head, and go on talking to you about the weather. And that, my dear brother, will be murder."

"I don't think we should tell her." Ennis agreed. "I think she'd figure out a way to have her accidently die, and I don't know what I'd tell Andi if I ever found out."

"You think she'd care?" He didn't know, but he didn't want to take the chance of her finding out. "Okay, I see your point. But mother fuck, you have no idea how much I'd like to be the one that sees her pay for this."

"Andi has to do it. And Jim. They have to be the ones that make her pay for the things she did to them. I'm not sure how — I'll have to think on that — but I think both of them will heal a good deal faster if we can let them settle this." Ennis agreed and helped him to stand up. "I want Mom and Dad to know this. They'll need to know to protect Andi when I'm not there. I have two projects in the works that I cannot leave going."

"I heard that she was going to work at the diner for Storm. I think they're both excited about it. Early morning shift to help out with the vets for Storm. I'll see if I can get someone to keep an eye on the place. I know a few people too. Not like Storm does, but I can call in a few favors." Mac knew a few friends too that would help him out. And Billy. "We have to get going. I told Mom that we'd run into an issue and that I would explain when we got there. And she said that Andi is sitting on the deck alone. Not doing anything, but when Dad went out to talk to her, she asked him to let her think for a while. Is she going to be all right?"

Yes, Mac thought. She was now. He was going to make sure of it. As they made their way to the grocery store to get the things on their list, he reached out to Andi and asked her how she was holding up.

I think I upset your father. I just needed a minute or two. He told her that he'd understand that. *This thing with my aunt, I've been thinking about what you said she was planning. How do you suppose she's going to sue you and your family? She has no money that I'm aware of. And according to what Riordan found, the house that she always told me was hers — and she only let us live there — was a rental. What on earth does she think is going to happen?*

Storm is looking into a few things. She has people who know people who know people. Mac had tried to make her laugh, but failed miserably. *Hester is not going to be able to do anything to us. I swear it. And anything she might make up, it won't stand up either. My family is a good one and there are no skeletons there. Hell, honey, Stormy is best friends with the president. He'll be in our corner.*

She didn't say anything, but he could feel her sorrow. When she told him she'd talk about it when he got back, he settled in the seat. Ennis asked him if she was all right and Mac told him he had no idea.

"I hope so, but I just don't know. This is nothing I've ever had to deal with before. And it hurts me that she's been hurt by all of this shit." Ennis agreed and they agreed to finish up and hurry back to the house. Mac thought that an excellent idea.

CHAPTER 8

Andi poured batter onto the grill to make a plate of pancakes before the diner opened. Billy was having some, as was the dishwasher—Danny from the Bakery. She had bacon going, some sausage, and was mixing up the biscuit batter for the other customers when Billy came back in the kitchen with her.

"Coffee is made. I got all the filters ready and full of measured coffee like you suggested. That'll save some time. I have a feeling that we're going to be really busy this morning." She handed him his plate of pancakes and told him where the meat was. "I called in Danny. He needed a minute."

He was just sitting down when Danny came in. The man was smiling, a rarity as far as Andi had been able to see. He asked her how long the biscuits were going to be, and she thought the man had a real sweet tooth when he pulled out a quart of strawberry jam to go with them.

"I can pop some in the oven to be done in about eight minutes." Rolling out a portion of the dough, she watched the two men eat. "You guys ever hear of moderation?"

"Sure, it's one of those diet words." Andi laughed at Billy as he shoveled a forkful of pancakes in his mouth.

When he was finished chewing, he turned to her. "You cook like this at home? If so, I bet Mac will be hitting the gym a lot more."

"I cook us dinner when Bethany and Rogers are out. Did you know that they were bears?"

Billy said that he did. She knew that Billy was something but not sure what, and that Danny was human. A human who had a lot of problems. Mostly in dealing with depression.

"I knew that, yes. Does that bother you?" She told him it didn't, but she was learning a lot of things that she'd not known before. "I'm betting you are. And these are the best pancakes that I have ever eaten. Hell, girl, you haven't cooked a bad thing yet."

"Yeah, you got that right. I tell you, a man could go on up to heaven if he knew this is what he'd be getting every day up there." Billy asked her how much longer on the biscuits. "I'm gonna get me some honey next time I'm in town. They got some next door, but I didn't think I could bring me in a gallon of it. Stormy, she uses it for some cookies she makes."

"I'll put honey on the list of things we need. I love honey and butter on a warm biscuit." When the timer dinged, she turned to pull the dozen warm breads from the oven. They were just the way she loved them, golden and flaky. The buttermilk on the top helped with that pretty color. "Here you go, boys, have at it."

There was a noise out front just as she was using the large round cutter to cut the batch of biscuits for the diner. Billy said he'd go look, it was more than likely someone wanting in early. When he was gone, Andi pulled down a large baking sheet and began putting the treats on it. Martha came in the room and started pulling on her apron.

Andi looked over at Danny and nodded to the door to get out. He slipped out the back door using his fingers to show her he was making a call.

"You just go on and get those done for me, Andi, and when the place opens up, I'll take over. I know you don't want me to lose my job, so I have to make myself useful. You don't mind, do you?" Danny was safely gone when she felt her heart pounding in her chest ease just a little. And she didn't know where Billy was. "What's the matter?"

"Where is Billy? I know he had all the work done out front before he sat down. Did he leave? And I thought you were told that you no longer work here?" Martha just waved her off and started mixing up pancake batter, having dumped Andi's mixture in the sink. "Martha, I don't think you're supposed to be here. I thought that Storm spoke to you."

"Oh that. She and I did talk, but I don't think she knew what she was thinking. She's had time to think things over now, and I just knew that you'd be here messing things up for me. I don't know why she hired you in the first place. I was doing just fine before you got here." The gun was pulled from Martha's apron, and she pointed it at her. "Now you go on ahead and finish up there and then I'll take over. I just can't lose my job. Medicines are so expensive, you know, and I really need the money. And when we get the doors open, you'll have to move Billy out of the way so no one sees him. I do believe he's dead."

"You killed him?" Martha told her that it was a misunderstanding between them and he'd not wanted to listen. "I'm going to call the police."

"Now you don't want to do that, Andi. I will lose my job for sure if you do. Make the damned biscuits." She felt someone touch her mind, and she was terrified that it was

Mac. He was on his way to Nevada today. His plane had left an hour ago. When he asked her what was wrong, she told him.

Get out. She told him that she didn't think that was possible, as there was a gun pointed at her. *Mother fuck. I'm calling my dad. I know he's pretty close. Don't get hurt baby. I can't…I'm too far away to help you.*

I know. I'm not sure, but I think she's nuts. Mac laughed and she smiled. Martha told her to get busy, they opened in ten minutes. *She's acting like this is all okay. That she's going to work here and that when we're ready to open the doors, she wants me to help move Billy's body out of the way.*

I can't reach Billy, so he's either unconscious or dead. Christ…. I don't…not even any of the people next to you. I don't have a connection to them. She said that she understood and finished up with the baking sheet. *Just do what she says. My dad said that he's on his way.*

Tell him to be careful. He wouldn't, she knew that. He'd come right in the building and get himself shot. And as scared as she was right now, she was more afraid of Ordan getting hurt. *Okay, I can't think with you and have her talking to me. I'll be all right.*

"I have to redo this every time, Andi. Your batter just isn't as good as mine. Don't make it up anymore. It's a waste of money." She told her that she'd not do it again. Then asked her to move so she could put the biscuits in. "Yes, this time it's okay that you changed things up. I wasn't here to tell you that we only serve these fools pancakes. Pancakes are filling and cheap. They do not deserve the best of anything. Did you know that Storm doesn't charge them for this food? I think that's the dumbest thing she's done. If she has that kind of money to burn…what do you think you're doing? You put buttermilk on those biscuits? I'm going to have to teach you how to make things with little cost, I guess."

"I think it makes them look pretty. But in answer to your question, I'm turning on the timer so I can put these in the oven." The knife slid into her apron pocket just as she picked up the first pan and slid it in the oven. The oven door was open and Andi thought this was the most surreal thing she'd ever done...baking with a gun pointed at her head. She also didn't want anyone else to get hurt, but she had a feeling that Martha wasn't finished just yet with her killing spree.

Just as she picked up the empty to put more bread on, she shoved it at Martha, trying to knock the gun out of her hand with the big pan just as the sucker went off. The pain took her breath away, but Martha was falling backwards and Andi knew that if she got up, she'd be as dead as poor Billy. Andi hit the floor hard, jarring her teeth together in the process, but was leaping up even as the gun was pointed at her again. The second time the gun went off, the shot went toward the front of the restaurant and she was glad that they weren't open yet. Martha pointed it at her again, and Andi decided that enough was enough. She was sick of people trying to hurt her. Picking up the first thing that she touched, the cast iron skillet jerked in her hand when Martha shot at her, hitting it instead of her again. Andi brought it down on Martha's head just as another shot was fired, and everything went black.

~~~

Ordan moved slowly toward Andi. She was hurting bad, he could see that. But she wasn't letting go of the skillet, and he wasn't fool enough to think that she'd not hurt him right now. Terror would do awful things to your mind, he knew. Reaching to his wife, who was just down the street with the aunts, he asked her if she'd called the police yet. Danny had gotten them out of the Bakery as soon as he could.

Yes. I have. And if you get hurt, I'm never going to forgive you. He told her that he was just fine; he was more concerned with Andi right now. *Is Billy really dead?*

I don't know, love. The only place I've been is in here in the kitchen. Martha is, that's for sure.

Ordan got down on his knees in front of Andi and said her name. "Darlin, you gonna have to give me that pan. They won't come in here and fix you up if you don't."

"She was going to kill me." He nodded at that, but didn't move to reach for the pan. He waited on her to hand it over. Stormy had told him to let her give it to him. It wouldn't get him hurt. "She told me that I'd have to help her move Billy out of the way for the customers before we opened, like it was nothing at all for her to have killed him."

The timer went off and he turned to look at the oven. Ordan asked her what that might be for, and she told him that he'd have to take her biscuits out for her, please. He had a moment of worry that she'd baked them up after killing Martha, but she spoke then.

"I set the timer and that sort of upset her for some reason. And the fact that I put buttermilk on the top of them. I think it makes them look all inviting, don't you? Then I put them in the oven and shoved the empty I'd picked up at her. If you would take them out of the oven before they get too done, when they help me clean this mess up, I'll get started on the milk gravy." Ordan nodded, somewhat relieved but very worried. "She tried to kill me. I didn't do anything."

"I know, sweetheart. Mac said to tell you that he loves you." She laid her head back but held onto the frying pan, like one would a weapon, handle first. Which, he supposed, it was for her. He heard the sirens now and hoped that there was an ambulance with them. He took the skillet and laid it beside him, trying not to think of the big split in the bottom of it and what had been done to put it there. "Thank you. I'll keep hold on it in case someone else decides to come in and try to take your job from you."

"Can I call you Dad?" He nearly fell back on his butt he was so surprised by her question. "You see, I don't have any good memories of my own father. And you and Bri are the nicest people I've ever met in my life. And you treat me like I'm a part of...well, I know that I am a part of your family, but you don't treat me as a...never mind. But I would very much like to call you Dad. And Bri Mom. I'd feel so much better if you'd think on that."

She put out her hand to him and asked for some contact. Ordan held her hand in his, feeling like he was finally helping her. He knew enough about crime scenes to know that you never touched anything. But he didn't figure that anyone would care if he'd taken the pan from her and held her hand. When she closed her eyes, it scared him a little, but the medics were making their way in and he thought she'd be all right. Mac touched his mind, and Ordan could hear the terror in his voice.

Dad, I'm taking the next flight home. Ordan told Mac he thought that was a grand idea. He wiped at the tears that threatened and told him he loved him. *I love you too, Dad. I'm so glad that you were there. Is she going to be all right? She told me that she'd been shot. Mom said that they just found Billy. Martha killed him.*

Andi has been shot twice. Once in the shoulder and once in the belly, but it's gone on through her, and the medic doesn't seem to be all that concerned. He looked up when he heard Storm and Riordan and stood up to hug them as he talked to Mac. *Asked me if she could call me Dad. Proudest moment of my day, I have to tell you. But she is talking out of her head a little. Worrying about the biscuits she's made. I don't think she realizes that she's been hurt all that bad.*

I'm coming home. Tell her that I'm coming home and I'll never leave her again.

Ordan didn't think that was going to be possible, but told him he'd tell her. But before he could say anything to her, the police arrived and ushered them out of the kitchen.

"She tell you anything?" Ordan nodded while he held onto his Bri. His knees had about given out on him when one of the medics started yelling something about losing her. He'd never been so afraid in his life. "Mr. Harrison, she's going to be fine. He only meant that she was falling over and he was worried for my crime scene."

"Well, I'm thinking he might have picked a better way of telling us all that, don't you think? Darned near had a heart attack. That girl in there is my son's wife, and it's up to me to keep her safe when he's not here." The officer nodded, and he looked for someone to take him away from the man. "You want to know what she said? She said that Martha tried to kill her. Told her that Andi should have understood that she couldn't lose her job."

"Mrs. Peterson had filed a complaint with the police department a few days ago. She said that Mrs. Harrison, Andi here, was trying to get her fired for being a better cook than her. None of us took it very serious, I'm sorry to say." Ordan said nothing. He'd bet from now on they did. "Ordan, I wanted you to know that there won't be any charges against her. It was plainly self-defense. If you talk to Mac, will you tell him that we will speak to him when he comes home?"

"I will. And thank you." The officer moved away and Riordan came to stand beside him and his mom. "I think she's going to be a might upset if those biscuits go bad. All she kept telling me was that she needed to get that mess cleaned up and the milk gravy started."

"Storm is having the aunts take them to the bakery to use. And Sally said she can make some gravy to go with them. Won't be as good as Andi's, she said, but she'd make sure that the men had their bellies filled up." Ordan nodded. "Dad, we should have been prepared for this. We were watching for her aunt and not Martha, and Andi got hurt."

"Son, you can't be there for everything. Martha was off her noodle and she'd have gotten past you even if you had all the guards around the place. And Andi is gonna be just fine once they get her in surgery. Mac is coming home and we'll deal with the fallout of this as it comes. But there was nothing any of us could have done to prevent this from happening." Storm made her way to them and she looked grim. "Go see to your wife. I'm afraid that she might want to pull her gun again."

"She loves the girl too." Ordan nodded. They all did. But Storm would feel guilty about Andi getting hurt simply because she'd told her that she'd be safe. "What do you suppose is going to happen now? I mean, there are two murdered people here."

"Nothing. Self-defense, he told me." Riordan nodded and put his arm around Storm when she came to stand with them. She told him that everything was taken care of.

"I've called a few people and they're taking care of the clean-up here. We'll close up for a few days, which I've been wanting to do anyway to have the kitchen fixed up. June said it needed an overhaul too." Ordan only nodded as he watched the gurney with the body bag being taken out. "Billy's parents are on their way to the hospital. They've been told what happened to him and, needless to say, they're devastated. Martha has a son and a daughter, and I'm trying to reach them, but they've never been very close to her apparently, and I'm not sure the numbers I have are working any longer."

"Andi said she told her that she and you talked and that it was a simple misunderstanding, and that she kept going on about her job."

Storm said that she'd talked to Martha and had told her she was fired. "She acted like everything was all right, but then when I was leaving, she asked me if Andi was still going to be working for her. I told her again that Andi was going to be taking over for her, that she wasn't to come to work anymore. That she no longer had a job." Storm shook her head as she continued. "I guess I should have seen it then, that she was unstable. But Christ, who would have thought she'd come here to kill them all? For a fucking job."

By the time Mac arrived, Andi was resting comfortably and out of surgery. They were going to keep her for a few days, just to make sure there were no complications, but everything looked good. Ordan looked around at his family as they stood in her room with her, and couldn't have been more proud of them at that moment.

"They're good boys, you know." He told his mate and the love of his life that he knew that. "I think when they all find their mates, we're going to need a bigger house. Most assuredly a bigger table. Do you suppose we should see about getting out the high chairs and baby beds?"

Ordan thought that an excellent idea. "I might even go out and dust off my tools, maybe make a few things for me and the grandkids to play on. I've been thinking we might want to put up a swing set, too, while we're thinking about them." He was warming to the idea now. "You know, we should think about a pool out back. Might take a lap or two myself, to keep me in shape to run after them all."

As they sat and quietly made plans, Ordan kept tabs on his sons and Storm. They really were good boys and he was very proud of each of them, how they'd come together for one of their own. When the captain of the police force and good friend, Oscar Miller, came in an hour after Andi had been put in her room, he told them what he'd found out.

"We've only just started looking through Martha's home, but I wanted to come and tell you that we've found some things there. Her son is on his way in, but I don't think he's going to be able to shed much light on the situation. And the daughter just hung up on me, telling me that she didn't care if her mom was dead or not. It meant nothing to her." He looked uncomfortable and Ordan was almost afraid to have him tell them what he'd found. "Her home has been...what I mean to say is that we've found...the things—"

"Oh for fuck sake, just tell us, Oscar." Ordan had to cover his mouth when Storm spoke. "Does she have dead cats hanging from the ceiling? Are there bodies all cut up in her fridge? What the fuck did you find?"

"Money. And a great deal of it. I would say, just in the kitchen alone, we've uncovered about fifty grand." Ordan started to ask him if he was kidding. "There are stacks of it everywhere. Some of it has been put in neat stacks in those zip bags, more still just with a rubber band around it. The canister set on the counter was filled with twenties, some of them dating back to the twenties and thirties. No change, as yet anyway, but cash galore. There was a stack of it in the fridge, as well as an entire top shelf in the freezer."

"And you say that it's all over the house?" For an answer, the officer pulled out his phone and let them flip through the pictures. Riordan laughed as he continued looking at them. "And where does this money go? I'm assuming the kids are going to take it."

"No. When I talked to her son, I mentioned that there was a large amount of cash in the house. He asked me if I knew what they were going to do with it, as you did. I told him that she was his mother, what did he want done with it, and he told me we could burn the house down with it inside if we wanted. He wanted nothing to do with it." Storm left the room when her phone rang, and Ordan wondered what had happened. The chief sat down then. "I had to convince him that she really was dead and that he needed to come up and ID the body. He said he would so his sister wouldn't have to, but I don't think he's planning to stick around."

Ordan just glanced at Andi, knowing that it would be the same with her should her aunt pass, or he thought when. The woman was going to piss off the wrong people sooner rather than later, and there would be hell to pay. He'd heard about the encounter Liam had had with her and had wanted to hunt her down for himself. But his son had taken care of himself and he supposed that was all that really mattered.

After they'd gathered their things up to leave, knowing that Andi was in good hands with Mac and the few guards that Storm had put around them, he drove him and Bri home. As soon as he was out of the car, he was heading to the work area that he'd played around with when he'd been younger. As he was thinking of all the projects that he wanted to get started on, he thought of the first time he'd been able to put something together that didn't look like a kid had slapped it together. A rocker.

"I still have it, you know. It's in Riordan's old room. I think he has some of his college things on it." Ordan looked at the love of his life and asked her how she knew he'd been thinking of that. "The look in your eye. You get that same look when I pull out the Christmas decorations and you find one that one of the boys made for you. Like the one that is shaped like a hammer that Liam made you one year."

"Yes, he was seven. I'd taken him with me to the hardware store to pick up something or another, and he found the instructions on how to make a birdhouse too. We spent the better part of the weekend going back and forth for each thing he'd find to make. I think we had more birdhouses than most of the whole block did." She pointed to just over his head and he had to laugh. His Bri saved everything.

There hanging above his head were ten of the worst looking bird houses he'd ever seen. Each of them got a little better, but all in all they were a mess. Only one of them had been painted; the rest had had things screwed or glued to them to make them decorative. He thought even the other boys had gotten in on the project by finding things to stick on them.

"When the grandchildren come, Ordan, I don't want to spoil them too much. And we will never go above their parents' heads on something that they said no to." He didn't even bother telling her she was full of malarkey, but listened to her as she said the stupidest set of rules he'd ever heard. "And we'll spank them when they need it."

"Okay, that one I can agree on. But you know as well as I do that we're going to spoil them as much as we can. When their parents say no, we're going to go it anyway." She said that they might make them upset about that one. "Okay then, we do it anyway if we don't tell their parents. I like that one. I think you can agree, we're going to have a blast with them. If they ever get here."

"I have no doubt that they'll arrive. But getting anyone to tell us that date might be a small problem." Yeah, he'd been hinting around about them for a week now and nobody was saying a word. "I guess we could go with plan B. And just start buying baby gifts for them and hope that they get it then."

"I love that idea, love. Very much so. And we'll start by giving some of their baby things to them. Starting with the rocker in Riordan's room." She nodded and smiled. "Yes, ma'am, we're going to be bouncing them on our knees by next Christmas."

CHAPTER 9

Mac wasn't sure there was a place to be had on this chair that wasn't uncomfortable. He'd tried stretching out, but his body was too long and he sort of hung out of it in strange ways. Not to mention, his long legs would take up most of the empty space between him and Andi, so that every time one of the nurses came in to check on her, he'd trip them up. When Andi giggled, he looked at her and straightened up so he could reach her hand.

"They said you'd be out for a little while longer." He had no idea why he was whispering—they were the only two in the room—but she pulled his hand to her mouth and kissed it, so he was okay with whatever happened now. "How you feeling? They said that you could have another shot for pain when you woke up."

"I'm fine for now. It makes me all woozy." Nodding, he held her hand tightly in his. "Did you hear anything more about Billy's family? Are they going to be able to stay here for a few days?"

"Riordan and Storm put them up in their house. It was a little hard to convince them they had plenty of room, but they've decided to stay. They're just waiting on his body to be released to them. And Ennis said it might be a few more days yet." She nodded and closed her eyes. She'd been doing that since everyone had left. Wake long enough to ask him a question or two, then drift off again.

"Did those men get their food?" He had to think what she meant, and told her that Lynn and Sally had taken care of them. "Good. Hopefully I can go back to work soon. I really like working there."

"Storm is having the place renovated for the moment. It shouldn't take more than a week, she said." Mac didn't tell her that they'd had this conversation before, and that he'd argued with her that she was going to have to wait a while before he wanted her going out again. "Craig was in earlier and said to tell you to have a speedy recovery."

"He's a nice old man." Mac had discovered that as well. The man was in his late eighties, yet lived alone and did all his own yard work, as well as cleaned up after himself. "Did he tell you that he's been eating at the diner since before we were born?"

"Yes he did."

Her eyes drifted closed again when he thought of his talk with Craig. He'd been in two wars in his lifetime, lost a son to one as well. His wife of nearly fifty years had gone to bed one night and hadn't woken up. He'd been doing for himself since. And he loved Andi as much as a man could a daughter, he thought.

"That woman of yours, she's about the sweetest thing I done ever did see. Talked to me like I was a person, too, and not some old fool like some of them younger people do." Mac told him that he was in love with her. "Well, of course you are. Plain as the nose on your face that you are. Couldn't have asked for a better mate either, I'm thinking. That Stormy, she's a pistol too. I'm sure your brother has his work cut out for him."

"Actually, he lets her do what she wants. He says it's because he loves her. But I think it's because he's scared shitless of her. So are most of us, if you want to know the truth." Craig laughed loud and for a long time. "How is it you know her? Stormy, I mean."

"She might not want people to know that she's army, but all you have to do is look to see it. So when I figured out what she was, I did some checking and found out a bit more. She's that woman, ain't she? The one that brought down them big wigs?" Mac said that she was, but she was very hush-hush about it. "I understand that. People, men mostly, will come here thinking that she's not all that. And when they'd find out that she's the real deal, then it'll be too late for their sorry asses."

Mac hadn't been sure what he meant and waited to ask him when the nurse came in to take Andi's blood pressure and vitals. As soon as she was gone, the door barely closed behind her, Craig started talking again.

"There are men who get in their heads that a woman just ain't as good as they are. And when they think one of them is about to show them, they gotta come on down and try to knock her around. I'm thinking if anyone ever tried that with Stormy, they'd be picking the pieces of them out of the carpet for a long time." Mac laughed and said he thought so too. "This one, she's gonna live a good deal longer if you convert her. I know you're a tiger and she will be too, but you should do it soon."

"I was going to when this whole thing with her aunt is over. I'm afraid that she'll try and hurt her while she's incapacitated." Craig snorted. "You don't think so?"

"I think if you have a weapon, use it. Don't wait for something to peck you on the head for you to remember you have a hat. Don't put your coat on after you've discovered that it's pouring down rain and you're standing in it. You have all the tools to keep her safe, use them before it's too late."

So now he was sitting here, thinking that the elderly man was right. He didn't want to have to wait for a peck on the head to remember he forgot his hat.

"What are you thinking on so hard?" He told her what Craig had said when she woke again. "I'd like that as well. Storm told me that if I was a tiger, I'd only have to shift and I'd not be hurting this much."

"I can get you something for pain." Andi told him she was fine, really, just making a point. "I don't want to hurt you baby, not with you being so weak right now. When you get healthier and are walking around…well, then we'll do it. I've never done it before, but Riordan has and he said that while it broke his heart to hurt Storm, she did well."

"Good to know."

When her eyes drifted closed again, he leaned back in the chair. He had other things to tell her, not important, but things she would have to know. After talking with Jim's doctor and with Ennis, he thought he had a better understanding of their childhood. And he wanted their children to have the best.

"Mac, let's have a baby soon. I want lots of babies to love and hold."

The statement startled him, and he watched her face to see if she was dreaming or really did want to have children. They'd not talked about them other than him to tell her what his dad wanted. When she looked at him, her face full of confusion, she asked him if he was all right.

"Yes. I think so. You want children?" Her nod had him smiling. "You want to wait on being a cat when we have them, or now? You're not in heat, how we create children, but we can give it our best try if you are set on it."

"I want to be able to beat Storm at something." Her eyes closed again and she yawned as she continued. "Do you think she does anything wrong? I mean, she can shoot, cuss, and cut a man to ribbons with her mouth or the knife I have never seen her without. I bet she even spits well. Don't you think?"

"I think you have her beat on a great many things. Like she can't cook anything, not even to boil water." Andi nodded. "And to me, you're much more beautiful as well. Not to mention, I don't think she can wear heels, much less those sexy boots I love you wearing."

"We should get married too." He nodded, telling her that they had the license when she was ready. "Now. Like as soon as you can get someone here to do it. I want to be your wife in real life, not just what people think."

He sat there for several minutes while she slept. He knew that he should get up and make the marriage happen, but for the life of him, he couldn't get out of his seat. He was going to get married. And soon. That looped around in his head several times as he watched Andi. When the door opened behind him and he looked at his brother, Mac got up and pulled Liam in his arms to hold him. Suddenly everything was just too much.

"You okay?" Mac nodded. "Okay, but you're kinda freaking me out a little. Tell me what's happened and I'll fix it for you, but you're scaring your little brother here."

"She loves me." Liam said he was pretty sure they all knew that. "She wants to get married to me...to me...and then have my babies."

"You're weird." Mac nodded and sat down. "Okay, the reason I'm here is Mom sent me. She wants to know if she can take a few things that are yours to your house while you're here. I'm not sure what it is but I'm to come here, ask you and get a key, then go over and help her load it up. I'd be more afraid of her than I am of anything coming in this place to get Andi. She sounded like she was on a mission and we'd better not fuck it up."

"Of course. It's probably some of my old clothes or stuff from school." He gave his brother his keys. "You should go with me in the morning, by the way. I need a bigger car and I don't want to have to go alone. Dad and Mom are going to keep an eye on Andi for me while I do it."

"Yeah, heard that you might be on the market for something like that. I wanted to ask you if I can buy your car. It's not what I want exactly, but I do need something smaller with all the trips back and forth to the office that I'm making. The truck, while fun to drive, is hard on gas and dating."

Mac thought of the first time he'd had sex with Andi in the front seat of his car and had to smile. Yeah, his brother would find out soon enough that things didn't work that well either. He told him he'd let him have it if he promised him that he'd go with him tomorrow.

As they sat there, whispering back and forth about this and that, Mac got a phone call that he took out into the hall to answer. The Stokes had been trying to reach him for a few days now, and he was running out of excuses to not talk to them.

"He's suing us. I know that it's not the way to start a conversation, but I thought I'd let you know that right up front." Mac asked Bryon who. "Elton...he's suing us for loss of wages. Anyway, we've talked to our lawyer and he said if we can prove that he was the reason our business was losing ground that it would go away. I'd really like for this to go away."

"I can't come out there right now. My wife is in the hospital." Bryon told him he was very sorry and asked him if he could do anything. "No. She'll be home in a few days, and if I come out there, then she'll have to come with me. I'm not leaving her again."

"I don't blame you one bit. So you'll come out? You'll help us?" Mac was cornered and he knew that he'd been neatly played. "We can put the both of you up and pay for all of your expenses. It would help us a great deal, and I know that we treated you poorly when you were here, but you did open our eyes to a lot of things."

"All right, but I'm not sure when. Like I said, my wife is still in the hospital." He made arrangements to call them in a few days. Before he hung up, however, he did ask about the lines and why they weren't running better with Elton gone.

"They have no idea how to run them. I mean, one of them told me that they'd only been showing up to work because they got paid, but Elton had refused to set them a job other than sweeping and making sure he was warned when you or my sister and I came around. He had the entire crew afraid of losing their jobs." Mac said he could see that happening and he had tried to tell them. "Yes you did. And you have no idea how much, every day, that we wish we'd have listened to you. Our shipping is so far behind right now that I'm terrified of losing more orders than we have already."

When he got back in her room, Andi was awake and eating a light dinner. She was joking around with Ennis, who had come by to check on her with Liam. When they left, he told her what the call was about.

"You should go out now, not wait. It's not like I'm going anywhere soon." He told Andi that he wasn't leaving her again, not ever. "And what do you think you can do while you're here? I think that even your mother would knock me around if I got out where I could be hurt again. How long do you think you'll be gone? Seriously, you have all the hard part done; you know what the problems are and you can go there, fix this for them, and be back in no time. You're going to just worry about them if you don't."

"No, I won't." But he would and he knew it. "What if some crazed woman comes after you again? What am I supposed to do with me all the way out there?"

"I'm pretty sure that I'd be fine. And if it makes you feel any better, I'll promise you I won't leave the house and I will be a good girl." He just snorted at her. "Okay, how about I go stay with Riordan and Storm? She's way scarier than anybody else we might know."

"True. And she does have a gun and isn't afraid to use it." He was beginning to see where she might be fine, and he did want to help the Stokes. "You promise me that you won't leave the house unless it's on fire? And you'll do what Storm tells you to do, no matter what?"

"I promise. Now make the flight arrangements and go. The sooner you go the sooner you can get back here and we can get married. This will give your mom some time to arrange things too. I'm sure she already has a list of things to do." Which was also more than likely true.

Riordan and Storm were leaving for China for a week and he didn't want to go. But his dad and mom said that they'd take care of her, and even Mason said he'd be hanging around as well. When they were all ganging up on him, Mac made arrangements and left that night. He hated to go, but she was right, he'd worry and if he left now, he'd be back all the sooner.

~~~

The house was quiet, and Hester thought it was the best sound she'd ever heard. Of course there wasn't anyone to wait on her, but she was content for now to do things for herself. It's not like it was a permanent situation. Andi would be here soon enough, and that idiot brother of hers would be so grateful to have a house to live in that he'd do whatever she told him. It was Hester's brother that was pissing her off.

Just this morning she'd gone to see him again. And unlike the first time, she had no issues other than her having to leave her cane at the front desk. Then she was shown to a nicer room and her brother was waiting. He still had that god-awful jumper on, but since things had gone so well up until then, she'd not said anything.

"How have you been, Hester? It's been a while." Hester told him she was having to do everything and that was pissing her off. "Well, when you live alone, those things happen."

"Where are your brats, George? I want you to make them come home now." He looked at her with that confused look on his face, and she smacked the table to get him to focus. "Andi and Jim. Where are they hiding out? I want you to make them come back to live with me in my house."

"I don't know who you're talking about." When his nose started to bleed, she watched as the officer in the room with him simply handed him a tissue. "Been doing that a lot lately. They say nothing is the matter with me, but it sure does make my head hurt at times."

"I don't care about your stupid head. You need to tell me where they are. I have things that I need to complete yet and they're keeping me from it. I do not like this, George, not one bit." He nodded but still looked confused. When she put out her hand to slap some sense in him, the officer only put his hand on his gun and she lowered her hand. Christ, it was getting so a person couldn't do anything they wanted any more. "Andi is supposed to have taken up with this man. What do you know about that?"

"I don't know anything." He got another tissue, and she wanted to tell him to stop this nonsense and answer her. "They're taking me to prison on Friday. To tell you the truth, I'm sort of looking forward to it. I've been there before, you know, and they feed you—"

"What the fuck are you talking about? You're not going anywhere unless I say you are. And you will not be going to a prison where I can't come and get answers from you. You tell them I said so." He nodded but didn't look inclined to do as she said. "George, so help me, I'm really going to lose my temper here if you don't tell me what is really going on with you."

"Nothing. I had a gun when I weren't supposed to and I hurt somebody. You know they told me that I couldn't have a gun when I got out." Hester sat up in her chair more and had to clench her hands together so she'd not hurt him. "You don't have to come up and visit me in the prison, by the way. I know that it's hard on you. But I did hear from a lawyer about the house."

"What about the house? That's my house." He shook his head. "Yes it is. When April passed, you said so long as I lived there and helped you with the children that I could have it as my own."

"I don't even own it, Hester. And now that the rent isn't being paid, I've been kicked out. And that'll mean you too, I guess. But anyway, you have ten days to get your things all bagged up. I'd help you, but—"

"Damn it, George, I will not be thrown like yesterday's milk out of my own home. It's mine, and I dare a soul to come and try to take me out. Tell me where that damned girl is and I'll make her pay it up. Fucking bitch should have been doing it all along." Hester wanted her cane. It was the best point-maker she'd ever used. "George, are you listening to me?"

"I don't know who you're talking about." He looked at the officer. "My head is hurting something furious. Can you make her go away? I just want to lay down."

"I am not leaving here without answers." But her brother did look ill. She snapped at the officer to help him, and all he did was open the door and tell her it was time to go. "I'm not leaving him. He has to answer me about those fucking little shits of his."

In the end she was escorted out and an ambulance was called for George. And no one would give her any answers as to what they'd done to him either. As he was being loaded up and taken away, she tried once again to get him to answer her.

"Where are they? You have to know where Andi is. I don't care about that retarded one, but Andi can get me money. I won't be thrown from my home." George started to sob, then, that his head was splitting in two that his brain was falling out. "Oh, don't be so stupid. You'd have to have something in there for your brain to spill out. Where is Andi, damn it?"

And now here she was with the mail from the last several days laid out in front of her, and she knew as surely as she was sitting there that someone was going to show up and try to take her house from her. The paperwork that she'd found in the dresser drawer had confirmed what George had said: the house was only a rental, and the letter he'd gotten a week ago said that they were going to evict them.

"Over my dead body." Hester sipped her juice and wondered where the hell those kids were. She would have thought that Jim at least would have come back. Him being stupid and all, he'd simply forget about her beating him every time she felt like it. "More than likely the fool forgot where he lived and here I am without nobody to help me with this. He'd find her. That boy could find her no matter what."

Kicking the mail to the floor, she nearly let it lay there when she saw the paper under it and the headline that seemed to blare out at her. Knocking the mail out of the way with her toe, she nearly spilled her drink all over her when she read what it said.

Cormac Harrison to wed Andi Collins in private ceremony. Picking up the paper now, she could see the picture of her niece standing alongside a handsome man. She read it three times over, but she couldn't find any mention of her name or that of George. Jim was saying that he was going to be attending the farce along with the Harrison clan. And right there, next to the groom-to-be, was the man that had assaulted her when she'd gone to see George the first time.

"She will not be marrying him. Not when they find out what I know." Standing up, she went to find her purse. There was nothing in it but her keys if anyone cared to look, but beneath the lining she had a small gun. Smiling to herself, she called her a taxi to take her to this wedding. The cab was pulling in the drive when she realized that the paper was two days old and that they were more than likely married already, since it had no date as to when the nuptials were to come about. Showing the paper to the driver, she told him to take her to the person's house on the page.

"The Harrisons expecting you, ma'am? They're a tight bunch and don't take to strangers just showing up." Hester hit him with her cane and told him to mind his own business. He didn't say a word again about being an unwelcome guest in her niece's own home.

If I play this right, she thought, *I can move in with them.* Or have them pay her. That sounded even better. That this rich husband—and she could tell that there was money to be had with this one—would pay her to keep quiet about what she knew about his new wife. She didn't know anything really, not even where she was, but she'd bet she could come up with a few stories that would make him pay her to keep quiet. As she was driven to the house, Hester started compiling a list of things she was going to tell the man. Yes, sir, she thought, things were about to get a good deal better for her.

CHAPTER 10

Andi was sitting on the front porch when the taxi pulled in. Dad was on one side of her, and her new brothers were all lined up on the other side. Not Riordan, of course. He was still in China with Storm and wasn't expected back for a few days yet. And Mac was still out west on a mission to save a company. He knew what was going on here, and while he wasn't happy about it, he knew she was as safe as she could be.

As soon as the cab rolled to a stop, Andi tensed up. Dad, always the calm sort, just put his hand on hers and told her they had it. She hoped so. Right now all she wanted to do was run and hide. But a standoff, as Bri had called it, was in order. She looked up at Darcy when he growled low.

Looking in the direction that he was, she could see the blood on the driver's forehead and wanted to go to him and see if he was all right, but didn't move. First of all, she was still sort of weak, and secondly, the man had told them what was going on with her aunt, as he was a tiger like them. She could not wait to get changed.

"There you are. Get in this cab and get your ass home with me. Christ, have you any idea what shit I've been going through with you three? Get in now, and I'll not take it out on you too badly what's been going on." Andi just stared at her. This woman had terrorized her enough, as far as she was concerned. "Did you hear me? Get your ass in this cab and let's be quick about it. I noticed that your new husband isn't here. Run off, did he, when he figured a few things out?"

"And what is it you think he might have figured out? That I'm related to you?" Andi laughed. "He knows, and despite that, he still loves me."

"Love? You have no idea what that word even means. He just wanted to fuck you and that's it. It's all men ever want from a woman. Get in the car." Andi told her no. "I'm sick to fucking death of people telling me no. And while you're at it, get some money too. I don't care if you have to sell off any ring he might have got you with. I need some cash and you're going to give it to me."

"No, I'm not." She stood up then, towering over her aunt as she stayed on the bottom step of the porch. "I'm not going anywhere with you. I'm not going to give you any money, nor am I going to let you hurt me again. You mean nothing to me."

"You don't mean shit to me either, but you will pay for being smart with me. And as for hurting you, I'll do what I want to you, and there ain't nothing you can do about it." Andi told her she was wrong. "Oh, am I? Does your new family know about the wolf you said you seen when you were tied up in the back yard? Did you tell them about that one? I bet you didn't."

"You mean that time you had me standing in the yard with only my panties on while you tried to teach me a lesson? Oh no, I didn't, but thanks for reminding me. This wolf came out of the woods behind the house and brought me a blanket to wear at night when it was cold, and he even brought me bottled water. I thought it wasn't real, that wolf, but he came to me again a few days later and begged me to run away, come with him to be safe. And if I remember correctly, you beat me harder when I told you about it. You are a horrible person, Hester. Try again to discredit me in front of these people, and I will hunt you down like the animal that you are. If we're going to tell tales about each other, then how about the time you tried to drown me in the tub when I was an infant? That is true, unlike your story." Hester just laughed. "You think it's funny that you tried to kill me?"

"No. I don't care what you think about shit like that. You didn't drown, mores the pity, but you are going to pay. Where is Jim? He's to get his ass home too." Andi told her he was safe. "He's never going to be safe. Not after what he did to me. He was supposed to bring you to me and he can't even be depended on for that."

"He's not going to be bothered by you again. And he's getting the help he needs too. From people that you should have got to help him long ago." Hester said nothing. "Did you know that there was an insurance policy that belonged to Jim and me? I'm sure you and Dad knew about it. It's gone a long way to take care of him and me."

"You'll be bringing that with you too. George tried to get it cashed in when you were little, but them damned lawyers, all fuckers if you ask me, said that you and that retard were the only ones that could collect on it." She looked at the cab, then back up at her. "I'm sick of standing here talking about this. Get in the car with that money and we'll talk when you get back home. I'm done with you, Andi; do as I say."

"I'm finished with you as well. You'll not be bothering me again, nor will you be hurting either Jim or I with your evilness either. So, if you know what's good for you, which I'm sure you don't have a clue about, you'd get back in that cab and go back to the house. At least for as long as you can. I guess you're going to be out of a house—"

"What do you know of my business? You talking to that owner? Telling him to do this? I'll have you know that's my house. I was promised it when I came there to help with you brats. You'll call him right now and tell him—"

"I own the house." Dad stood up then and walked to stand beside her as he addressed her aunt. "As of last week when I found out where you were living. One call and I owned it. And in a few days, when you're out, I'm going to have the entire place burned to the ground. The fire department is going to use it for practice and then clean up the area for me."

Her aunt took a step toward her, and Ennis shifted. She wasn't sure if the rest of them had or not, but she could see him as he stood on the ground in front of her, between her and her aunt. Hester nearly fell trying to get away from him, fear written all over her face, and Andi laughed at her. Running her fingers though his thick fur, she watched her aunt while she tried to get her purse open. But Donald, the cabbie, simply walked to her and jerked it out of her hands. The cane too.

"What do you think you're doing? Unhand me." He pulled the gun out of the bag and handed it to Aedan, along with the cane. "Give that back to me this minute. I will not have you stealing from me. I'll call the police."

"You go right ahead and try." Andi glanced at Dad when he spoke. His voice was dark, heavy with something scary, and she saw his own cat race along his skin before he spoke again. "You don't have a phone, first of all, and even if you did, it would never make it to your ear. I'll have your throat torn out before you even get it dialed."

His cat moved again. This time even her aunt couldn't have missed him. When she backed up, falling against the car twice before she got to the door, Donald stood waiting with them as Hester got inside without saying a word. He looked at them as they stood there.

"You know as well as I do this isn't the end." Andi nodded. "When she comes back—and she will—she's going to try and kill you and the rest of this family. Might do you a world of good if you just took her now."

"Too many people know her. Might not care for her and wouldn't necessarily mourn her death, but we gotta do this the right way so's as it don't come back to bite us in the ass." Donald turned and told Hester to shut up when she told him to get in the car. "You be careful there, Donald. I don't want you to get hurt again by her. And I thank you for the warning that she was coming."

"You tell Mac that I got his butt."

Andi nodded. She waited until the car was out of sight before she moved back to the chair. She'd been on her last leg and had been afraid that she'd collapse where she stood if her aunt hadn't left when she did.

Mom came out of the house with a glass of juice and her pain medications. Andi thanked her and took both. She didn't like the way they made her feel, but she was willing to feel dizzy for a time rather than sore again. She was helped into the house by Liam and taken to the couch, were she'd been when the call had come in. Closing her eyes, she let the drugs take her away, for a time anyway.

~~~

"We have to hire more workers, don't we?" Mac said that they'd need at least two or more people to catch them up in their orders if they wanted to keep them. "I can do that, but who do we hire? I don't want another Elton on my lines, if it's all the same to you."

Mac started to tell them that they could get some temps in to work. They were usually trained on production lines even before they came to work. But something that Ennis had said to him made him pause while he gave it some thought.

"A few days a week my mom goes and works at the nursing home. She's not a nurse, but she does know a little about crafts. Anyway, she goes there because she gets bored at home with all of us gone, and it gives her a little extra 'mad money,' as she calls it." Mac was warming to the idea. "What if—and this would have to be worked out—what if you hired some of these older workers part-time, to help them out, and get you some much needed workers? Mom told me that most of these people are just as bored as she was, and that they worked outside of the home just to have something to look forward to. I even think there's a tax break for hiring them as well."

"I got something on that the other day. Let me look." Noreen looked at the papers on her desk and pulled one out. "Here it is. I think this was put out by the local adult living home near here. Some man by the name of Jennings came by and told me that they'd do about anything within reason."

As the three of them went over the regulations of hiring people with some disadvantages in what they could lift or do, Noreen was making a list of things that they had to improve on in the building itself. Which was very little, as the upgrades had been done when their father had gotten ill.

"This might work. I'm sure there are any number of people out there that could use some extra money too." Bryon was ready to go out with his car and bring them in, he was so excited. "I'll make a few calls in the morning and we'll see how to get this going. You know, the extra hands will be great, but I wonder how many of them might have a few good ideas to help us out too. Christ, Dad would love this."

As Mac made his way back to his hotel for the night, he felt better about coming out here. Andi was fine, thanks mostly to her being able to stand up to her aunt for now. His dad was happy too that he'd gotten to witness it, and Mom was going on and on about how happy she was that they weren't upset with them. He had to admit, however, coming to the house to find not just a baby bed and some of his old toys, but a new mattress and baby items, had thrown him just a little.

"We need a grandchild, Mac." He was on the phone with his mom as he packed to come out here, asking her about the items when she said that to him. "My friends all have grandchildren of their own. And here your father and I are, six grown boys and not a baby in sight."

"You should have one then. You and Dad are still young." She had sputtered for two minutes before he laughed. "Actually, Andi and I have talked about it. Once she's converted we're going to try. I know that Storm and Riordan are waiting, but we have decided that we don't want to."

"Don't you dare tease me, young man. I'm in no mood to be made fun of." He assured her that he wasn't. "You really are? You're going to have a baby soon?"

"As soon as we can after she's a tiger. I think it would be easier on her, what with all this other crap going on, if she were a tiger and not human when she gets pregnant." His mom squealed out her delight and then told his dad, who promptly got on the phone to verify it.

"A grandson would be good, but I'd take either right now. I can take a little girl fishing as well as I can a little boy." Mac assured him that it might take a few years for that to happen. "Yeah, well, you don't know me very well, then, if you think I can't handle a little baby and a fishing pole. She'll love it as much as any little boy would. Maybe even better."

"I have no doubt, Dad, none at all. But, just so you know, if you treat her girly, I think Storm will kick your ass." His dad laughed and said he believed she would too. "I'll talk to you about it when I get back."

His dad had assured him that he'd keep an eye on Andi and that nothing would happen to her on his watch. And from what he'd heard today, that was just what his dad had done, kept an eye on her. Laying in his empty bed, he reached out to Andi.

How are you? Getting the rest you're supposed to be getting? She told him she was. *Good. I want you rested and well when I get back.*

I talked to the man designing the new diner today. Storm asked him to come by and see me if he had any questions. Did you know that she's expanding the dining area to be three times as big, and the kitchen is getting bigger as well? Sheesh, she'll have to hire more people to handle all that. Mac asked her if she was worried about going back. *I don't think so. I mean, I'm nervous. But I don't think it'll be too bad. Everything will be new and fresh, so that's the way I'm looking at it.*

Good. I heard that there is going to be a huge walk-in too, so you can have fresh veggies for soup all the time. And Craig said to tell you when it opens again, he's going to be the first in line. Andi laughed and told him that he'd been out to see her. *He's a very nice old man. I think he might be sweet on you too.*

He told me he was. Said that I reminded him of his wife when she was alive. Mac had told her about Craig and his life, what he knew of it. *He wants a job. He said he can run the cash register as good as any kid. I'm going to talk to Storm about it when she gets back.*

Did Dad tell you that your father is going upstate to the prison in the morning? She said that he had. *I had Ennis go out and tell Jim. He seemed genuinely relieved about it.*

Me too, if you want to know the truth. If he's there, I don't have to worry about him getting out. It's happened before. He knew it had. Storm had told him that he'd gotten out twice when he should have been sent up. *My aunt isn't going to go away, is she?*

No. Not easily, anyway. You do know that you handled her just fine, don't you? You stood up to her again and that had to piss her off." She told him it was hard, almost as hard as it had been when she'd been in jail that time. *You keep it up. If Storm had been there, you know that she would have shot her, don't you?*

Yes. She would have had her bleeding on the ground even before she got out of the cab. And Donald did great in letting us know she was coming. I'm not sure how it would have gone if she had surprised us. He told her that they would have circled around her and she would have been just fine. *When are you coming home? I know that I wanted you to go, but I really miss you.*

I should be able to leave here tomorrow night. I talked them into hiring senior citizens to help out on the lines. We have to find out what that entails, as well as how to schedule it to work. Bryon said that he could buy a bus to cart them back and forth to work, and his sister is game for it as well. He smiled when he thought of how on board these people were now. *I have to write up a report on what we're doing to make improvements, as well as what I found when Elton was still working here. The other employees are glad he's gone, but have no idea how to do their jobs now for the most part.*

They talked a little more about the lines and what there had to be done to make them viable again. She suggested that they hire a cook to make sure that there were foods there that they could eat, that vending machines might be dangerous for a few of them.

I miss holding you. I never realized how lonely a bed could be without you here. Her sigh made his cock stretch. *I would like nothing more than to take you right now. Tell me, are you naked, Andi?*

Yes. I just got in the tub. There are bubbles all over me. Even my nipples are hard because of them. Christ, he thought, he was going to die here. *Are you hard, Mac? Is your cock thick like it is when you fuck me?*

He pulled his cock free of his boxers and fisted himself. *I'm hard as stone, and precum is dripping from the tip just thinking of you all wet and dewy in the tub. What are you doing?*

Touching my pussy. He nearly jerked his cock from his body. *And my nipples ache to have you suckling them. When you do that, you have no idea how wonderful it makes me feel. I get wetter just thinking about you nibbling on me.*

He fisted his cock tighter. His balls were tightening up, filling to be released. When she moaned again, he did too, thinking about her fingers in her pussy. Her voice was coming to him in short pants now, and he knew that he wasn't going to last much longer.

Oh, Mac. I'm so hot right now, my pussy is ready for your cock. He was ready for her too, and hated the distance between them. *When you eat me as your cat, his tongue fucking me, I feel like he's going to touch the back of my throat, he's so deep. Mac, I'm coming.*

So did he. His cum shot up a foot before coming back down on his body to burn him. He came a second time when she screamed out her release to him, and he felt his body tense up again when she cried out his name for the third time. As he lay there, stroking his cock, he closed his eyes and wondered how he'd gotten so lucky with her.

I'm worn out. He laughed and told her that he'd probably sleep better too now. *Good. I've never done anything like that before. It was so...intense.*

You did it very well. He laughed. *When I get home, I want to watch you do that same thing. I want to watch your face when you come.*

I'd love to see you coming too. I want to taste your cock, too, like you do my pussy. His cock stirred, and he wondered if she was teasing him. *We need to get a vibrator.*

Christ, woman, are you trying to kill me? He fisted his cock again, thinking about her using a vibrator on herself. Then he thought of him using it on her. *I'm going to go shopping before I get home. Thinking about eating you with one in your pussy has me hard as a fucking stone again.*

I want to come again. He closed his eyes, thinking of seeing her there, sending what he was thinking to her. *Oh Christ, yes. More.*

Every dirty thought he'd had since he was a teenager, he put her body and face into it. She was standing in the woods naked, tied to a tree while his cat took her. Her body bound to the bed while he fucked her. Thoughts of taking her in the shower, the hot tub, and anyplace else he could take her ran through his mind and into her. And when she screamed again, telling him through their link that she was coming, he felt his cock erupt and he nearly passed out, it felt that wonderful.

Long after she told him that she was going to bed and good night, he lay there thinking of all the things that he wanted for them; not just sex, but just life in general. He wanted children, as much as she did. He wanted safety, which was something that he was going to take care of soon. And he wanted to spend the rest of his life with her. Growing old and feeling good about each other just the way his parents had.

Rolling to his back, he looked up at the ceiling, wondering about her cat when he converted her. What their children would look like when they came to them. How they would be as parents too. Smiling, he felt good about life in general and could not wait to get back home again to start it. Life, he knew, was going to start looking up. More so than it did already.

CHAPTER 11

Hester sat in her recliner and watched the door. She had her gun at her side as well as two pistols in her lap. There was no one coming here to take her home, by God. And she'd kill the first person that tried to do so. Her fucking brother had promised her this place when she came here, and he was by God damned going to make it happen for her. The phone in her hand, the one she'd picked up today, was still playing music instead of giving her the answers that she wanted. There was going to be hell paid for that as well.

"Hello, Mrs. Casey. What can I do for you today?" She wanted to tell the woman she could eat poison and die like the rest of the fucking cunts in the world, but she needed her right now and decided that she'd be a little nicer than she might have been otherwise. "I'm to understand that you wish to speak to your brother. I'm sure you were made aware of it, but he's no longer —"

"I know that, you fucking bitch. I want you to connect me to him anyway. There has to be some sort of connecting shit going on so you all can talk to each other. I'm not stupid, you know." The woman asked her to not use such language. "I will use any fucking language that I want to use. I demand that you connect me to him now, bitch."

"You want to talk to me like that? When you want something from me? All right then, we'll work this your way. He's not here. They chained his ankles and hands together yesterday, after doing a thorough cavity search of his person, and took him to the prison, where, in my opinion, he should have been years ago. He went in a large van with other people of his like. Where I'm sure you might end up if you keep talking to people as if they are beneath you." Hester had opened her mouth to blast the fucking bitch when she continued. "You have a really nice day, and think about all the times he's going to get a prick up his ass. Much like the rod you have up yours."

When the line went dead, Hester had a good mind to call her back and give her a piece of her mind. But she didn't. Not that she didn't want to, but the fucking phone told her that she only had seventeen minutes left to make calls on it. And she didn't want to waste her breath talking to some woman who for all Hester knew had slept her way to her position. Who was more than likely at this very moment down on her knees in front of the man behind the glass giving it to him.

"People and sex. What the fuck is wrong with you that you feel the need to have it?" Hester had never enjoyed the coming together of two people. Her husband had had numerous affairs when she told him that he couldn't stick that nasty thing in her again. And Hester had been just fine with it. Any woman who would let a man do that to her was lower than a snake as far as Hester was concerned, and she had it on good authority that sex was the ruination of the world. All it begat was brats, and she hated them as much as she hated sex.

Getting up, she made her way to the door to peek out to make sure no one was sneaking onto her property. Yesterday someone had come up on her porch and stapled a notice to her door saying she had ten days to vacate the premises or she could be considered trespassing. The nerve of some fuckers.

Going to the kitchen with her weapon, she pulled out one of the many cans of soup she'd had stashed in her room over the last months. Hester had been hoarding food forever, but lately she'd been putting back things like water bottles and canned meats too. She knew there was a day of reckoning coming and she was going to be prepared for it. She had a feeling that she was going to be putting up a siege, and now she was glad that she had seen it coming.

"Damned people. Making things hard on me." As the soup simmered on the stove, she glared at the contraption that George had stolen off the back of the truck for them. The microwave was a work of the government she'd told him when he bought it in, to kill them by putting them waves in their bodies so they could track their every move. He'd laughed at her. She realized then that he'd done that a lot when he'd been here.

"Sure, I know that the government is tricky and always trying to take things from us, but this thing is to make life generally better for us. Cooking food is quicker with one of these things. Let me show you."

"You'll do nothing of the kind. You keep that thing and whatever shit that comes out of it away from me. I don't even want to have you running that contraption when I'm in the house. You hear me, George? I'll hurt you bad if you do." He asked her how he was to use it then, because she never left the damned house. "Good. You might just thank me when everybody that has one of those things is like the walking dead people because the government has fried up their brains for them, and you and me are just fine."

She wasn't sure that it had ever been used since that day. Even looking at it now, she was amazed at how new it looked and wondered how much she could get for it. Not that she needed the money. She had her pension as well as her stash in her room, but it never hurt to have a little more.

When the soup was finished, she moved it off the burner and poured it in the bowl she had out for it. Hester enjoyed her own company. She was the smartest person she knew, and hated being around others who were just too stupid to learn to breathe on their own. Not even her brother could hold a candle to her wealth of knowledge. And she was street smart too. Knew more than most people who even had a college education. And Hester prided herself on her knowledge about the government too.

They were out to get them all. Control them in any way that they could, and would just as soon kill anyone off that knew what was up faster than even the biggest criminal. Hester also knew that they were running tests on people. Changing them into things that weren't right. Messing with the things that God had put here. Like them damned people that her niece was with. All of them monsters.

"One day that's gonna bite them in the ass too." As she crumbled her crackers in the soup, she smiled at the thought of one of them big nasty beasts that they made with their labs and shit, and hoped that one day that she'd hear about how it had eaten all them fuckers at the White House. "Serve them right too, fucking around with things that ain't got no business messing with. I'll be the only woman alive with nary a thing to do with them monsters and still living in my own home."

She moved between the kitchen and the living room all throughout the day. Twice someone pulled in the drive and she waited, her gun ready to shoot whoever came on her property. But all they did was use her drive as a turnabout, and she was going to put a stop to that too when this shit was done.

The ringing of her phone startled her so badly that it was almost done ringing before she remembered she should answer it.

"Hester?" She sat down on the chair as her brother's voice came through the line. "Hester? They said to call this number, that you was looking for me. Hester, where are you?"

"I'm here. Yes, I've been trying to reach you. Where the hell have they taken you now?" He told her that he was spending the next five years in the big prison. "What for? You tell them I said to let you go or I'm gonna come there and show them what it's like to take what don't belong to them. I can't be dealing with this right now, George. You done left me in a jam, and those damned kids of yours ain't helping me."

"Kids? I don't...I can't talk about them with you. It hurts my head something painful." She told him he'd better damn well talk to her about his kids. "I can't, Hester. Makes my nose bleed and my head twirl around like one of them topsy turvy things I had as a boy."

"You always had the best toys, and I will not be put off for this. I want you to tell me how to get them back here. I know that them people are hiding them away from me. I want you to get here so I can make them mind." He told her that he wasn't going to help her. "What do you mean, you're not helping me? You most certainly will. Get your ass here right now, George, or so help me I'm going to make you regret it for the rest of your short miserable life."

"I like it here just fine. I don't want to talk about no kids, and I don't want you to come and try to get me out of here." She started to tell him he was fucking insane when he spoke again. "Yes, I like it here just fine. I got me three straight meals a day, a bed that don't snap springs in my private parts when I move, and I can watch all the television I want. I'm happy here."

"I'm not happy, and you know what happens when I'm not happy, George. People get into trouble when that happens. I'm telling you right now, you will come here and help me. Or so help me, I'm going to go there and beat you to shit for treating me this way." He told her he was sorry. "You have no idea what that's going to mean on you when I'm done. Get your fucking ass back here and help me out of this shit you put me in."

"I'm done with you, Hester. You have a fine life. And when I get out, if I do, then I'm not going back there either. There is a buzzing in my head that tells me that if I do go back to there, I'm not going to be long for it." He told her again that he wished her the best of luck with it and hung up on her.

It took all her willpower — and Hester prided herself on her power of the mind — not to toss the phone to the wall and have done with them all. There was no hope for her brother right now, but when he got out she was going to teach him a lesson or two that he'd not soon forget. She'd done it before when he'd had it in his mind that she should do more around the house. This time he'd not soon forget she was ten years older than him. And, as such, deserved to get what she wanted.

"They'll all learn that I'm superior to them. And when they get that in their thick fucking heads, I'm going to never let them forget it."

~~~

Andi felt her body come apart. Even as she screamed out her release, she had a moment of worry. She'd been alone when she'd come to bed. Mac was still helping his clients. But looking down her body, she saw him there, his big cat, between her thighs as he ate at her pussy over and over. She curled her fingers into his thick fur and held him to her as he slid his tongue deep inside of her.

He loves the way you taste first thing in the morning. All dewy and wet for him. She cried out again when Mac, in her mind, brought her again. *Come for him, baby. Fill him with your juices so I can have my turn.*

"Fuck me, Mac. Please. Fuck me." He growled low, the sound of it making her body tense up for another climax. And as she released again, she felt something powerful and magical tighten the room, and looked down at Mac, her man, as he grinned at her from where his cat had been. "Please. I need you."

"And I you. I'm going to feast on you. Then I'm going to fuck you until we're both completely satisfied." His tongue licked over her pussy, tickling her clit as he did so. "This is the best part of having you sleeping naked. Christ, never wear clothing to bed again. Come for me, Andi. Come so I can have my fill of you as well."

His hands were everywhere. His fingers were touching parts of her she was sure she'd never touched. He made her scream, beg, and cry. Mac was relentless, loving, and kind. When he nibbled on her clit, sliding his fingers in and out of her pussy, she came again, screaming so loudly that she was sure she'd be hoarse for a week. And when he lifted his body from hers, Andi knew that he was only getting started as he made his way up her body, biting and nipping at her skin as he did.

"When I got in this morning, I thought about letting you sleep, maybe even taking a short nap with you. But you were naked. Christ, it was all I could do not to take you then." She touched him, his hardened nipple, as he passed her, his muscles tight in his arms as he held himself over her. "You're in heat, love. If we do this right, you'll conceive my child."

Her body seemed to hum at his words, come alive with the need to fill her body with his child. As he kissed her, deep and lovingly, Andi thought of his baby, their child, growing within her.

"Yes. I want that." He touched his cock to her pussy, the heat of him nearly consuming her with it. "Give me your child, Mac. I want to love your child as much as I was never loved and cared for."

He slammed forward, taking her breath away and bringing her to peak again. When he started pounding her, his entire body seemed to go between human and cat, his beast—as he called him—claiming parts of him and her as he fucked her through three more powerful climaxes. When she knew he was close, his cock taking short, hard punches at her, she tilted her neck and gave him her throat.

"Take me. Now, Mac. Make me whole." The cat in him growled and Andi felt it to her toes. And when he snapped his mouth over her throat, she knew the kind of pain that she'd never felt before. Pain that had her pulling back from him even as she held him to her.

She knew from talking to Storm that it was painful. That the bite was necessary, but it hurt like a motherfucker. As he continued to take her, giving her as much of him as he could, she thought of being a cat, a tiger, and knew that it was going to be all worth it.

As he emptied deep inside of her, his teeth tore at her flesh again. Even as she knew that she was getting weaker from it, he moved down her body again, this time as his cat, and bit deeply into her belly. Holding onto her consciousness, she told him how much she loved him. Andi never lost sight of the fact that she belonged to him and only him.

Screaming again, this time in agony, she waited for him to take the final bite, the last one that would hopefully change her over. As Mac's cat tore into her leg, Andi felt herself slipping. There was nothing left in her to scream with. All her energy was in just staying awake to tell him that she loved him. When his cat lifted his head from her leg and whimpered, she pulled him close to her with the last of her strength and closed her eyes. She'd either die a very happy woman or be a cat in a few days.

The room was dark when she woke. The heavy furred animal at her side had her curling into him. But the voice beyond the darkness had her turning in that direction. When the light came on, she stared at Storm for several seconds before the other woman smiled at him.

"He's been here, as his cat, for two hours. He thinks he killed you." Andi asked her how long she'd been out. "Yeah, about that...not so long. You were, like me, supposed to be out for a week, they said. I didn't think that shit worked for me, so I was awake in a few hours. Same with you. You've only been out for about four. Good job, that."

"He was afraid he'd killed me? Why?" Storm said she had no idea what went on in the mind of a man when everyone could see that it had worked. "I'm a cat? I'm really a tiger."

You really are. Andi looked down at Mac when he spoke to her. *Get rid of Storm and we'll just cuddle here for a few minutes before I take you in the woods and run you down.*

Andi looked at Storm to tell her that…well, she wasn't really sure what to tell her, but she was leaving anyway. When she paused at the door, she turned to look at her and Mac. Andi knew right then that Storm would be her best friend for the rest of her life. She had no idea why that thought popped in her head, but once there, she knew it was true.

"Congratulations, and good luck. Don't forget, it's easier to walk on two legs than four when you get out there. Just saying." Nodding at her, Andi looked at Mac when the door closed behind her.

"I'm a tiger. Have you seen her yet?" Mac said that he had not. That she was going to show him now. "I have no idea how to even attempt that. What do I do?"

Think of her. But —

Whatever else he was going to tell her was lost as her cat just consumed her. Every part of her body seemed to be turning inside out, but not in a painful way. As she sat there, her body humming with her newfound power, she blinked several times as his cat stood next to her.

I was going to say, wait until you have us a clear path to get out of the house, but you were too quick. I usually love that about you, but now…. Well, we have no one to open the door for us.

Oh. I guess I should have waited a minute or two. He laughed and rubbed his long body against hers. *I can feel that all over me. I mean, like you're stroking me from the inside out.*

I will be soon enough. Once we get out of this house, I'm going to show you how to run, leap over things, and generally enjoy what you have become. He moved to the bedroom door and waited. She started to ask him how to change back when the door opened, and Riordan was suddenly there laughing. *Lucky for you, Riordan was still here. Or we'd have to replace everything in this room.*

What do you mean by that? She looked around the room as he answered her. *Oh. You mean cat sex isn't as pretty and maintained as human sex? Good to know in the event that I'm a cat and we're in close quarters, and I have a sudden urge to jump you.* Laughing, she watched the two men as they stared at her.

As soon as Riordan moved back from the door, she took off toward it. It felt strange at first to walk on four feet rather than just her two, but she got the hang of it soon enough. But when she came to the stairs, she stopped and looked down at them. It was a scary thought, going down them like this.

"Move down them one at a time until you get the hang of your new body." She looked up at Riordan as Mac streaked past her to the front door that was standing open too. "You need to exchange blood with all of us now. So that we can converse in the way of our people."

The way of our people? He laughed again and rubbed his hand through her fur. *You're a sap; has anyone ever told you that?*

"Yes, daily. So, how is it you can talk to me this way, I wonder?" She didn't care and took off, carefully, down the stairs. Moving out of the doorway, she heard Storm laugh and suddenly just didn't care. As soon as she felt the earth beneath her feet, it was all she could do not to dance at the feeling it gave her.

It only took a few moments to find which direction Mac had gone. His scent, like his cologne, seemed to call to her.

After nearly tasting him on a few branches, it became less easy to find him by scent. It was as if he were teasing her into looking harder for him. Just as she came upon a stream of fast moving water, Andi stood as still as she could when she saw the stand of deer that had been there the other day. They were just as alert and cautious, but today there was one less of the babies.

I think he was killed several days ago when they were crossing the road to our land. A car hit him but didn't stop. I didn't know if it was their baby or from Riordan's property. But the reason they haven't taken off with you standing there is that they can't smell you as yet. If they did, they'd be gone in a minute. Lifting her head as slowly as she could, she looked for Mac. *I'm to your left. You'll have to be very still and concentrate to see me. It's the reason we're marked the way we are.*

It took her ten minutes. When he asked her repeatedly if she needed help in locating him, Andi told him no, she wanted to find him on her own. But as soon as she saw him, his tawny stripes blending in so well with the surrounding grasses and scrub around him, she watched in marveled awe when he came closer to her.

If there was a word for the way he looked right now, Andi had no idea what it might be. Amazingly beautiful. Sexy beast. Breathtaking form. All these combinations of words, but not a single one seemed to fit him.

I love you, Cormac. With all that I am, I love you. He paused coming toward her, his sleek body standing so still he looked like a part of the world around them rather than a man who turned into a cat. *You are the most wonderful thing that has ever happened to me.*

And you to me. I have loved you for all of my life, I think. Only waiting on you to come to me so that I could give you my heart. Her own heart seemed to melt at his words. *Now run, Andi. We wish to chase you, then fuck you.*

She took off, startling not only the deer that were there but a raccoon and a few squirrels too. The woods, it seemed, were alive with life. She was amazed at all the sounds she could hear as well. Even the flapping of the wings on the birds overhead.

Andi loved how she felt, the way her body seemed to know just when to jump, when to land, and how not to hurt herself when she did. Just as she was congratulating herself on her ability to adapt so well, she was knocked to the ground so hard that she tumbled ass over head three times before she stopped. Then Mac was standing over her. When he ordered her again to run, she stood up and rubbed her body against his, feeling the same connection to him as she did in the house.

I want you to take me. He told her that it wasn't like that when his cat had his fun with her. She more than likely wouldn't enjoy it. *But you will, and that's what matters.*

As soon as she rubbed her body to his other side, he bit down on her shoulder and mounted her from behind. It was strange and weird having him do this, and her cat seemed to take exception to it. Snarling and trying to throw him off, she tried to calm her, but it didn't work. She was pissed.

His cat, bearing her down to the earth, sank his teeth harder into her shoulder when she tried to get away, and she finally sat down and stopped moving. He couldn't take her and that seemed to piss him off more.

He's going to hurt you. She told him he could try. There was humor in his voice, like he was enjoying the fight as well. When she was able to break free of him, his cat snarled at her as she took off again, and this time she decided to be the aggressor rather than the victim.

Twice he walked by her. She wasn't sure if he was teasing her again or hadn't found her. But when she was knocked down again—this time he wasted no time in entering her—she submitted to him. There was no other word for what happened between the two cats. He took, she let him. When he finished, Andi snarled at him and Mac laughed.

I told you it wouldn't be the same. I'm so sorry about that. But he needed your cat to submit and when she was did, it was good. Shift, love, and we'll make it worth your while.

She thought of her body, the one that seemed to be right there for her, and felt her human self come around. When she was standing there, naked and ready for him, Mac's cat knocked her to the ground and buried his head between her thighs.

He wasted no time in bringing her three times. Each time she thought she couldn't take any more, he'd nip at her flesh, her clit or her thigh, and she'd come, screaming again. But when she begged Mac to come to her, his big cat melted away under the man she'd come to love. As soon as he was deep inside of her, his cock filling her like the cat never could, Andi watched him, his cat just on the surface of him, as he made the most glorious love to her.

As they lay there, each of them holding onto the other, Andi wondered if they had created a child or not, and what would it be like to love someone as much as she did Mac.

CHAPTER 12

Hester slipped up behind the man who pulled out the newspaper and caught the door just before it closed up tight. Smiling to herself at her win, she pulled out the paper and stuck it with the rest of her stolen items in her large handbag. She'd eat well tonight, she thought with a grin.

Two days ago she'd come upon the idea to change her appearance so she could go into town. It had taken her the better part of the next day to come up with a suitable outfit to change herself, but in the end she'd been quite pleased with it. Then yesterday she'd walked around the neighborhood, not too far from home in the event some fool came to run her off again, and hadn't been recognized by a single idiot. One man had even asked her if she would help him gather wood that was free for the taking. Like she would do a thing for anyone that lived on her street. After telling him to fuck off, she made her way back to her house and made her plans to make a trip to the store and other places that needed taken care of.

So today she'd gone to the store first, getting the much needed supplies that had run low over the last few days. Expiration dates hadn't been considered when she started hoarding her foodstuffs, and she knew it was something to do with the government trying to control them again. They were putting shit in the food so that when they decided it had been not used soon enough or they wanted the consumer to spend more money, they set off the charges and the food would spoil. Fuckers. They wouldn't beat her at this game. Hester knew she was much smarter than any of them anyway.

Of the fifty or so cans of soup she'd had in her room and other places in the house, forty-four of them had been tampered with. The lids had even popped off on a couple of them, leaving her a mess to clean when the smell died down. There was going to be hell to pay when her niece and nephew came home. And her brother wasn't going to be allowed in the house once he got his shit together either. Fuckers, all of them.

All in all, it had been a very profitable day, she thought as she made her way back to her home. She had meat now...not a lot, but enough to sustain her for a few more days if she was careful. Vegetables that were as fresh as she could get them, and some milk. None of that non-dairy shit either. Wholesome milk for her coffee, which she had managed to get as well. She'd even been able to get in and out of the post office without being seen, and had cash money, too, to put by in the event she had to venture out again before she was able to bring the kids to heel. Pulling out her paper, she sat down on the bench under the big elm and opened it up while reading the most recent propaganda that it was spouting.

The headlines on the front page were the same shit. Someone was pissed off at someone else. There was war going on here or there. Hester knew that it was all lies; there were no wars going on, only people wanting the money spent on them. It was like when they said they put a man on the moon. Hogwash, all of it. Why on earth would anyone want to travel all that way just to walk around in some sand? They want that kind of shit going on, just travel to the beach and do it. She turned to the next section to read the obits and news there. Usually they could be counted on to get that shit right.

Nearly choking to death on a grape she'd pulled from her bag, she read the first headline there three times before she could get the stupid fruit dislodged enough to catch her breath again. There was no fucking way this was true. Looking around, she spied another newspaper stand machine and went to it. Not even waiting on someone to buy a paper first, she paid the fifty cents and pulled out another paper.

Another Harrison Bachelor is Off the Market. It was the subline that had her seeing red. *Cormac Harrison has married Andi Collins in his parents' home.*

She'd told that girl no and here she had done just the opposite of what she'd told her. That damned girl was going to pay for this; Hester would make sure she paid dearly for it. She was going to beat her within an inch of her life.

Hester looked around for someone to confirm what she was reading and, of course, they were too busy with their mind sucking phones stuck to their faces or in their laps while they entertained themselves on them. Porn, she knew that was what they were seeing. Everyone was looking at porn and she knew it.

Hester stormed up to one man who seemed to be talking to himself, and she jerked the tiny thing off his ear. She'd thought it was an earring, but apparently it was a talking thing and he was pissed off at her because she'd ended his call. He screamed at her for two minutes before she snapped at him to shut up.

"And fuck your call. Where did this news come from?" He looked at the paper she was shoving in his face, then down at her. The smirk on his face had her wanting to wipe it and him off the face of the earth, but he crossed his arms over his chest like he knew what she was thinking. "Who wrote this shit, and how to I get it retracted? I did not give anyone the say so to print this crap, and I want to know how to get it taken out of the paper."

"You don't. I mean, it's true, so why would you anyway? Andi is a nice girl, and Mac is very—"

Hester hit him, just drew back her fist and slammed it into his face. As she was walking away, she heard him screaming something about lawyers and owning her, but she knew he didn't have a leg to stand on. As far as he was concerned, he'd been hit by a fucking man, not a woman like her. He'd have to find her, wouldn't he?

"I'm going to kill her if she thinks this is funny. I'm not the least bit amused. She's not going to be getting married to nobody. Not so long as there is breath in my body, she ain't." Taking the shortest route to her house, walking through yards instead of the walkways, Hester came upon the cruiser long before she did her home. And when she saw them bastard suits on her porch with Andi and three other men, she didn't even think about what she might say to them, but walked up to them and reached out for Andi.

Her hands come up empty when she went to snatch the girl bald. Her arm that held her big bag was pulled up behind her back, and all her things dumped on the ground before her. Andi was still standing there when she glanced over at her, and she would swear the bitch had the nerve to be laughing at her. Hester saw red so deeply she was sure her eyeballs were bleeding from it.

"Let me go, you motherfucker. I'm going to have a word or two with that ungrateful cunt there." There was laughter again, this time from all of them, and Hester tried to jerk free of the man but he only held her tighter. "You're going to pay for that, you son of a bitch. I'm going to beat the living shit right out of you as soon as you set me free. Let me go, you moron."

"I don't think so. I sort of like having you where I want you. And if you think my wife is going to let you touch her now, you're stupider than I thought you were. And that's saying a lot. Hester, you're going to hurt yourself more if you don't settle down."

Hester started stringing together curses at the man that she knew was making no sense whatsoever, even to her ears. "You slimy cock hammer shit fuck pecker-head. Let me go right now, or I swear to Christ that I'm going to hurt you in ways you cannot imagine." Jerking on his grip on her only did what he'd said it would and hurt her worse, and pissed her off to the point where she no longer cared what she said. "You prick-eating douche knob fucker pompous fart lover, let me the fuck go."

"My goodness, Hester, where did you learn those words? Oh, I know, down on the dock where you lived." Hester looked at Andi and ordered her to call her aunt. "No, I don't think so. Not anymore. That is a term of endearment, or at the very least, respect, and since I have none whatsoever for you, I'm not going to call you anything but your given name. I do not like you, much less feel any sort of endearment toward you. But I will say that you have been very busy, haven't you? Calling the prison to harass them, stealing from the local stores, even going so far as to hitting an off-duty cop when you didn't like the headlines of the paper. You're not going to be able to get out of this very easily this time, Hester. There are witnesses to your dirty deeds."

"You had me followed? There is no way you knew it was me." Her hat was pulled off her head and tossed at her feet. "You didn't know it was me, I know you didn't. You're lying, you fucking bitch. And don't think I've not been making a list of shit you owe me for too. You're going to be chained to the floor like I told your daddy to do years ago. You'll never see the light of day again. And this marriage you think you have? That'll be over too."

"I'm pregnant too." Hester forgot about the man holding her and jerked her arm in a way that she saw stars when it pulled at her. She didn't have to have no doctor degree to know it was broke, either. She felt it all over her body. But she'd be damned if she'd let them know it. She was made of better stuff than any of these fuckers were. "And so you know, I've been changed into a tiger as well. I'm about as happy as a woman can be. You should try it sometime. It's an amazing feeling. Being happy, I mean. Not the tiger part. You're not fit for that, I think."

"You'll be changed back too when you get your ass back in that house. There is no way I'm going to have a monster in my house." She tried to use her arm, just to prove to them that she wasn't hurt, but tears filled her eyes when it moved.

As she sat down on the porch, her arm throbbing like a bad tooth, she wondered what the fuck was wrong with these people. They were acting like there wasn't a thing wrong with this shit. Changing into monsters wasn't natural, she knew this. The government did this. Well, she'd show them. Pulling her things to her the best she could with her one good arm, she told them what she thought of all of them.

"You're all gonna pay for this shit. See that I don't bring a hurt down on you that you'll feel for years and years. Once I get me in my house, I'm going to be making me some calls, see if I don't. I've had enough of this bullshit, and I'm getting that useless daddy of yours back here too. I knew I should have killed him when I did your mamma. Things might have been a little different for me had I did it. But now here I am stuck with doing all this shit on my own." She realized that no one was speaking and looked up at Andi when she thought about what she said. "You don't think she died all on her own, do you? Had to teach that boy a lesson too. When I told him to leave her to her own business, all he did was mope around like he was lost because his mommy was so sick. She wasn't sick, she'd done birthed a fucking brat. One I was gonna have to kill too."

"You killed my mother? Jim told Mac that you did, but...you actually let her bleed to death while he begged you for help?" Hester snorted her answer. "What kind of monster does that? And why? What did she ever do to you?"

"Monster? I'm no more monster than any smart person who knows that kids are going to ruin this fucking world. Look at you. Standing there with your hooking boots on, your too tight sweater. When you come to live in my house, and you will, there will be changes made. And that babe? Well, it's a good as gone too. The first thing I'm going to do is have someone come in and exercise you back to the other fucking dumbass you were. Then you're going to set to doing what *I* want from then on. I've about done with you."

"Hester Elizabeth Collins Casey, you're under arrest." She looked up at the cop in front of her and spit on him. Hester no more believed in the authority the cop might think he had over her than Andi was thinking she going to go on like she had before. "That's not going to win you any kind of brownie points with us downtown, you know. You and your brother, you're quite a pair, aren't you?"

"Fuck you. You get his ass on back here too. He's got some things to answer for like the rest of them. I'm going home. Andi, get rid of them monsters right now and get in that house. You have a lot of work to do." When she felt herself being lifted up, her arm making her sick it hurt so badly, she screamed at them to let her go. But all they did was take her to the cruiser that was still sitting on her front lawn. Hester reached into her pocket and pulled out her gun just as the cop, the filthy piece of shit that was telling her she had rights, was shoving her into the back door.

Hester thought about killing the cop, but she knew for some reason that she'd only get one chance at this before they tried to knock her down again. So she thought of that fucking niece of hers and wished that Jim, the retard, was here too so she could kill two birds with one bullet.

Turning toward Andi, doing something that she should have done years ago, Hester pointed the gun at her and smiled. As far as she was concerned, Hester was doing the world a favor by taking one more monster out before it was able to breed. But before she could do more than just point it, Andi was gone and in her place was a huge fucking monster. A fucking tiger, of all things, that the government had sent to kill her with. Even as the cat leapt at her, Hester fired her gun until all it did was click. Then it hit her. The big cat took her to the ground.

~~~

Bri watched her daughter-in-law closely. There were times when she wished she could read minds. This one time she wished that with all her being. The girl was hurting, anyone could tell that, but what was paining Bri was the fact that the Mac and Andi had been so happy a few hours before all of this.

"You know, I don't know if I'm ready now to be a grandma. I never realized how much work there was in preparing for one." Nothing, not even a blink of her eyes, Bri could see. "My mother-in-law told me once that had she had any idea how much work grandchildren were, she'd never have had children. She wasn't a nice person."

That was the wrong thing to say, she supposed. Her mother-in-law hadn't been mean, just too...well, forthcoming, about everything. And she did have an opinion on everything, it had seemed. When Holly, Ordan's mother, was upset about something or she didn't care for a person, you knew it. And so did anyone around her.

"Ordan and I have been dusting off the rocker in the house and getting out the play pen in hopes of having a grandchild soon. Just didn't know it would be this soon. Why, I've barely got one pair of booties knitted. I'll have to work harder, I suppose." Bri wanted to shake the girl and tell her that she'd done nothing wrong, but Mac had told her just to talk to her, she'd come around. "Of course, I do have all of my boy's things. I gave some of it to them recently, but there are a few things that I was holding onto. Silly, I guess, but they're warm with memories I have of them."

She looked around the room where the police were talking to Ordan and Mac, everyone trying to sort out what had happened to Hester Casey. They knew, of course. Her body had been ripped to shreds by Andi, her cat protecting what she'd considered hers. Bri wished now that she'd not recognized Hester when she'd been in the store earlier today and let the boys know she wasn't home. Things might have gone on longer, but Andi wouldn't have had to do what she'd done.

"Did you know that when you have your baby, it'll look as human as every other child in the nursery? I knew that, of course, but I didn't know if you knew or not. When I had Riordan, I was terrified that someone would tell me I had to leave the hospital and take my son with me. Of course, back then it was harder to get around being a shifter. Not like it is today. Some people actually think it's sexy, I heard." Bri was babbling, but it was that or beg the young woman to talk to her about what was bothering her. "I've also gotten out the Christmas ornaments. I know it's not quite Thanksgiving just yet, but I just had a need to get them out and sort them for the boys. I guess men now, but they'll forever be my boys. I thought about giving them their own, but I so love the ones that they made me. I have treasured them for years."

"I've never had a tree. Not a real one anyway. There might have been one before I was born, but of course I don't remember it." The words, spoken softly, broke her heart all over. "My aunt said it was the work of heathens, and my father went along with whatever she wanted. He was afraid of her, I guess. Jim...one year Jim drew a tree in class. It was before they kicked him out, but he made this beautiful tree with too much glitter and so many small puffs of cotton on it that it was hard to see the green of it. To me it was the most beautiful thing I'd ever seen. We hung it in our room, behind the closet door so that no one would see it. It's strange how those sort of memories pop into your head at the strangest times, isn't it?"

"It doesn't get any better as you get older, either. But as for your brother's tree, that was lovely of him. He wanted to give you something that every child should have had. He's doing well in the place he is. Did Mac tell you?" She said that he had. "What did you do for gifts that year, Andi? I'm assuming that he helped you with that as well."

"Yes. His was stolen, of course, but I really didn't care then. It was a way of life for us. He got me a candy bar. And wrapped it in the Sunday funnies so it would be bright for me, he told me. I gave him a box of crayons, used and some of them were broken, but I knew that he'd like them. Jim used to like to draw." Andi smiled then, a painful smile but one nonetheless. "It was the only time in all my childhood that we had gifts for each other. That year, I mean. The tree hung there for months after that. I'd go and look at it when he'd have to beat me for something that Father thought of. Or he'd be in trouble with the law again. Then Hester found it and...."

Bri took her hand in hers. "We'll have a lovely tree at our home this year. Not that we don't have one anyway, but with two more to add to our family this year, it will be a grand celebration. And just thinking about the new baby for next year makes me giddy with excitement. A summer baby will be so wonderful to play with. And by the holidays, we'll be watching her get excited over the lights and glitter." Andi nodded and put her hand over her flat belly. "She didn't harm the baby; you know that, don't you, love?"

Andi nodded but held her belly. Bri wanted to tell her that she could hear the child's heartbeat should she want to. Hear that it was strong and steady while nestled there. But she held her tongue, waiting for the girl to get her bearings back.

"She wanted to kill me. Hester, she wanted me dead. I've never...she really hated me." Bri felt her heart tighten up in her chest again when she thought of what that monster had done to her Andi. "Just pulled out the gun and shot me until it was empty. I had no choice but to attack her. What if she had hit any of the others there?"

"You did well, my child. You not only saved my sons and husband for me, but you got rid of that horrible woman in the process. No one is blaming you at all for it." Andi tightened her grip on her hand before letting it go. "Andi, Stormy said that when she and Riordan come home, she's going to teach you how to use a gun."

"She told me. I don't think I want to learn though." Bri could understand that. She hadn't been sure she wanted to either when the lessons started, but she was liking the way it made her feel when she could shoot the heart out of one of those paper targets. "I told Jim she was dead."

Bri knew that as well. Mac had told her that she wanted to do it herself and had called the home where Jim was staying. Apparently it had gone a great deal better than any of them had expected.

"He is all right with it, isn't he?" Andi nodded at her question. "I'm to understand that she wasn't all that good to him either. She should never have been in that house with you children, much less your father being there. I've never heard of a group of people less suited to having children than the two of them."

"She killed our mother. Hester acted like it wasn't any big deal for her to have done it either." Bri knew that as well. One more reason to rejoice in the death of the monster. "Jim had told Mac about it, and he told me this morning. I never knew it was true, but...she really killed her and made Jim clean up after her."

"Your...Hester didn't deserve you or Jim. And your father should have been horsewhipped when he let her treat you as she did. I swear to you had I known any of this was going on, I would have gone there and shot her myself. The nerve of some people. Did she not have any idea what she was throwing away?" Bri looked at Andi when she laughed a little. "There now, there is no more grieving for that horrid woman. And we're going to settle on what to have for dinner on Thanksgiving while the men are busy sorting out what happened."

"I killed her. I think they all know that." Bri said that she was glad for it, but the police weren't going to fuss about that. "What will my children think when they find out that I killed two people? They're going to wonder why I did such a thing."

"They're going to think that they have the bravest mother in the world. And that they want to strive to be just like her when they grow up. And if you give me a granddaughter, just one, I will tell her all sorts of things about her father that will make her laugh and enjoy him all the more." Andi slid to the floor and laid her head on her lap. Bri felt her tears threaten again as she touched her soft head with her fingers. "I love you, Andi. You and Stormy have done so much to bring me such happiness."

"I love you too, Mom." Bri felt tears burn her cheeks as they slid unchecked down her face. "When I have this baby, I want you to be there with me. I need you there with me when we come home too. I have no idea how to be a good parent. My own childhood should tell you that much. But I will love the baby. No matter what."

"I'd love that very much. And I know you will. You're going to be a very good mother because of how you were brought up. You'll want to be better, and you will be." She wiped then at the tears as she continued. "You should name her for your mother if it's a girl. I think that would be wonderful, don't you?"

"Yes. I have to think on it though. I'm still getting used to being pregnant." Andi looked up at her then. "Whatever it is, you guys are going to have a lot of fun with it, aren't you? I can see you guys taking the baby to the zoo and stuff even before it knows what an animal even is."

"Nonsense. Your children will be born knowing everything. And what they don't know, we'll teach them. We're going to enjoy that too." Andi smiled, the first one she'd had since they'd brought her here an hour ago. "You're going to be just fine. You know that, don't you? No one cares a bit that she's gone, nor how she came to be that way."

"She hated me." Bri nodded again, wishing she had been able to show the woman the error of her ways. "And Jim. I'm going to see him soon, talk to him now that he's in a better place."

"Good for you." Andi laid her head back down, and Bri looked over at her husband and smiled when he winked at her. She loved that man more than she ever thought possible.

And I love you as well, my dearest heart. Nodding, she held the woman on her lap, telling her things about Mac that she'd not thought of in years. Yes, she thought, having a grandchild in the house was going to be so much fun. Just seeing her son trying to figure it out was going to be well worth it.

CHAPTER 13

Andi moved out into the lobby to see who was left to feed. The restaurant, Home Cookin', had been reopened for nine days so far, and it was doing so much better. There was more seating than there had been before. The kitchen was well updated, and there were more workers too, to accommodate the lines of people that came to eat every day.

Craig was here, she saw. He'd been staying until she left for the day, or so Dean—Dean Burns, the new place manager—had told her. And there was the gentleman that had been here daily for about a week now. She smiled at him when he waved her over.

"Hello. Did you get enough to eat?" He told her that he had had the best lunch he'd had in all his life. "Well, I don't know about all that, but I'm glad that you came in."

"If you have a moment, I would like a word with you, Mrs. Harrison." She still had trouble remembering that was her name now and asked him to call her Andi. "All right, Andi. If you have a few minutes, I have something I would like to talk to you about."

Sitting down, she noticed that there was a large envelope next to him and a satchel. Not the kind that some men carried, that they thought made them look cool, but one that was used and well taken care of. And she'd bet, very old. Craig came over then and poured the man a cup of coffee and handed her a glass of tea.

He'd been doing that lately, helping out in the restaurant a little here and there. Mostly with the coffee pot or refills on drinks. She thought it made him feel useful for his meals. Not that it mattered to her. She just loved the elderly gentleman. When he nodded at the man in front of her, she felt safer for it, thinking he'd given his approval or something.

"I came here a few days ago to see what sort of person you were." Nodding, she looked around, wondering if this man, like a few others in the place, thought she was fair game or something because she worked here. Flirts mostly, but she wasn't used to being treated that way. Mostly it had been the opposite. "My mother was Martha Peterson. I'm Drew, and my sister's name is Lizzy."

She started to stand, then sat down hard. Her knees were shaking and she was afraid if she had to run, she'd fall. But he put his hand over hers, and she looked up at him when he said her name softly. He looked...well, crestfallen. A word that she'd never used until just then.

"I'm so sorry about your mother, Mr. Peterson. I have no idea—"

He cut her off by raising his other hand. She wanted to tell him that she'd not meant to kill her, not meant to do anything at all to upset her, but he held her hand in his for a minute longer before he spoke.

"She was a horrible person. Not just to you, which I'm sure she was, but to us—my sister and I—as well. I'd like to, if you'd let me, share a story of her. Something that I think will bring home how grateful I am that she is no longer with us. I know that it sounds horrific to you, even to my ears it does. I know that it's not right, but once you hear this...I hope, anyway, that you'll understand why I came here. Why I feel this is the right thing to do."

Nodding, she watched his face. He was struggling with something and she wondered if he knew about her own father and aunt. If so, then perhaps he'd think her as horrible as he thought of himself. When he let go of her hand and clasped his together on the table, she felt herself relax a little. She wasn't afraid, but she was worried about him.

"My father, my step-father really, left just after Lizzy was a little over two years old. Barker—his first name—Barker told me once that he'd rather live with her to see we were taken care of than to let us be raised without love. But in the end, it became too much for him as well." He smiled then, but it was a bitter one that never reached his eyes. "I was about five then, nothing much to speak of, but terrified of my mother all the same. When I think on it, even then I knew that my mother had run him off. Drove him away more like it. Just as she had us. And I think, even now, that she was relieved when we left her. Lizzy and I left when I turned eighteen and her just fourteen. We never once, in all the rest of our lives, ever had a thing to do with her."

"She was...difficult, I guess you could say." He laughed, and it sounded harsh and cold. "I tried very hard to do what she wanted. Storm talked to her too. She was just too set in her ways to let anyone but her do things. It became apparent that the restaurant would fail if she stayed. But that day she came here, I had no idea what was going on until she'd already killed poor Billy."

"The police said they think there might have been others. They're looking into a few missing persons in this area. I've given them a list of people that were in and out of our lives when I was younger. I have no idea who else might have come to harm from her. I'm not sure what that might mean for them. With her dead, I'm sure that they won't be able to charge her with anything. But, like I said, I have no idea." Andi had heard there were two bodies found on the property, one long dead, the other as recent as last year. "But they told me that the contents of the house belonged to me and my sister. Whatever we wanted out of it, we should take. There was not a single thing there that I thought either of us would want."

"The same with me and my father's home. He told the attorney that he wasn't coming back. That if we wanted to tear the house down, he didn't care. Of course, the house belongs to someone else, but everything in it has been burned. But I understand there was a great deal of money in your family home." He nodded, looking away from her to the outside where snow was just beginning to fall as several store fronts put up Christmas decorations in anticipation of the coming holiday season. "You said you came here to see what sort of person I was? I don't understand that."

"When we were living there, Lizzy and I, the house was cold during this time of year. She'd never turn the heat up past fifty, and if the temp got up above fifty-five outside, she would open the windows to the house to air it. I think it was to kill us both in our sleep." Andi said nothing, not even sure what to say to that. "One year, when I was ten and it had been a particularly hard winter for us, I asked for a pair of boots. Nice ones, ones that didn't come from the free clothing drive that the churches had yearly."

He sat there, saying nothing for several minutes. As she watched him again, Andi could swear that the man had aged a great deal. He'd been worn before, the best word she could think to describe him, but now he looked ill with his age and the burden of being Martha's son. Andi figured that having a support system, like the family that she now had, was what got her through all this. And the fact that she had something special to look forward to.

"The house back then was much like it was when the police went there. I mean, right down to the same shitty furniture. Money in stacks everywhere too…not nearly as much back then, mind you, but there all the same, and none of us were to ever touch it." He smiled then, the same sad one from before. "Some of it in neat piles on shelves. There were plastic bags of it stacked up like books on a shelf, each of them dated with the amount within. The freezer in the basement held no meats or vegetables, but bags of cash, hordes of it from her childhood until forever."

"Ordan said that the officer that was first on the scene had taken pictures of it. He thought no one would believe it if he hadn't." Drew nodded. "He also told him that your mother was on welfare, that she got free food handouts when they were available, as well as clothing from the drives at the local churches too. She would be the first in line when there was a free meal, and told everyone that would listen to her that she wasn't making it, her meds and bills were too much."

"Why spend her own money when she could get so much for free?" He laughed a little. "We had no things in our home. And what I mean is we had no television sets, no radio, or foo-foo things, as she called them. We had a couch that held us when we wanted to sit, and lamps, one on each end of the couch, to see by. A table with three chairs, three plates…well, you get it. There was no money spend on things that were not necessary, and she had the final say on what was necessary, let me tell you. And even then, they had to be something that was needed or die."

She waited for him to explain the boots. Andi had no idea, but she had a feeling that they were going to be the reason for his hatred of his mother. Something that only she, as a person with the same sort of feelings for her father, would only understand about him. As he sat there, Craig filled their glass and cup. He said not a word, but she could tell he was worried for the man. As soon as he walked away, Drew began again.

"They were on sale, these boots I wanted. They were new and not full of holes. I'd not have to wear plastic bread bags on my feet to keep my feet dry. But she said no. She told me, over and over, that I wasn't to have them. The shoes that I had were sufficient for me. They fit, did the job that they were required to do, and that was enough for her. But I wanted them, wanted them in a way that only a child could want, I suppose. And the money was there. We could see it. Why not just buy me the boots to keep my feet dry? I didn't understand. Not then, and certainly not now." He looked at her then. "Lizzy served as lookout while I took it. I wanted them that badly, you see. I never thought she'd find out. Yes, there would be dry feet, but that would make her happy when I wasn't sick with a cold again that winter, I rationalized to myself. So while I climbed to the highest shelf in the living room, Lizzy watched for her. When I had two twenties, money from two different bags of cash, I hid it in my watch pocket and knew that by that time next week, I'd be wearing new shoes, as would my sister. Then when they were purchased, I would put the change back, not having any idea what things really cost as we never bought anything, and I felt like Mother would think me brave and smart for doing the right thing."

"She knew." He nodded and sipped his coffee. Andi was sure that he wasn't tasting it, the bitterness of the memory was taking that much of him. "What did she do? Whip you? Beat you? I'm betting she didn't think you were brave at all, did she? Nor did she think you very smart."

"No, neither of those things. When I returned from school that next day, Lizzy was tied to a chair, her pretty face bruised and beaten. Her left eye was swollen shut, her arms bloodied from the beating that she'd gotten with the flyswatter that was her favorite type of weapon. I should have run, I suppose. I knew what that I'd been caught, but I couldn't leave my sister to take it alone. The next thing I knew, I was falling forward, the pain in the back of my head too much for me."

Tears fell from his eyes. His handkerchief came from his pocket then, and he wiped at them as he looked around. The man was in so much pain that Andi could feel it. Almost touch it. When he looked at her this time, she wanted to go to him, to hold him in her arms. Not the man he was, but the child that he'd been.

"When I woke, I was tied to the other chair, as my sister was still. We were at the kitchen table, tied there like a morbid surreal dream. I could see that she'd found the money. It was in a plastic Baggie, taped to the table in front of me. Lizzy had one in front of her as well. It wasn't until I tried to move, to see if I could try to reason with her — my own mother — that I realized that this was well beyond what should have happened to a child who only wanted boots. But there wasn't any reasoning with her, and I should have known better. I just wanted to let her know that my sister had had nothing to do with the money when she hit me with the stick in her hands. Over and over until blood ran freely down to my hands. My arms burned in pain...the switch hit me in the face too. I screamed around the cotton taped in my mouth then, begged her to no avail to let Lizzy go. But she would hit her too. Never asking a question or saying a word, just beat us until there was no skin that she'd not touched." Andi reached for and took his hand in hers as he continued. "Mother tied us there for five days. Saturday through Wednesday without food or water, hitting us when we were awake and telling us how much she was disappointed in our transgressions against her. Our transgressions against her for wanting something as small as a ten dollar pair of shoes for each of us. Money, as far as I could see, was in great amounts all about the house, yet it did us little good for it being there. For five days, five full days, we were beaten, screamed at, starved, and given no breaks. We sat in our own piss and crap for all of those days, beaten and shattered."

He sobbed, great gulping sobs that tore at her. Even as she held his hand, he cried. Andi wanted to go and find his mother's grave, dig the woman up, and kill her again. This was beyond cruelty, what she'd done to her children.

"It was still there." It took her a moment to realize what he'd meant. "When we went to the house, the police took me there to show me what they'd found; the money in the envelope was still taped there. The freshness of the tape told me that she'd kept it there to show whoever might come by that her children had disappointed her. It was the same two twenties too. I could never forget the numbers on the bills."

"Oh, Drew." He waved her off, his heart broken because of that woman. "I'm so sorry. So terribly sorry for everything."

~~~

Craig sat across from Andi. He had waited a good long time after the younger man left, but here she still sat, holding onto the envelope he'd given her...well shoved at her would be a better description, but here she sat all the same. He touched his fingers gently to her hand and she looked at him, dazed.

"He said that he didn't want it." Craig nodded, knowing that whatever had the boy coming in here to talk to Andi about had been hard on him. "He said to use it how we saw fit. That he knew we were working on a shelter for vets and the homeless, and that he thought we could use it to make a difference. He wanted it to make a difference in someone's life as it never had his."

"I'm a guessing that it's money he gave you." She nodded and pushed the thick envelope to him, and he pushed it right back. "You thinking of not taking it because of what his momma did to you? Or did he say something that makes you think she's coming back for it? She ain't, I can tell you that."

"No. That's not it, but there is...have you any idea how much money he gave to us?" Craig had an idea it was a lot, but said nothing. "There is over seventy grand in cash there, as well as ten checks made out to me for two hundred and fifty grand each. He said that it was all tax free, the cash. That's well over two million dollars that he said he didn't want."

"Two million, five hundred seventy thousand." She glared at him. "Well, I was making sure you know how much you're dealing with, darling. But I'm sure if he hadn't wanted you to have it, he wouldn't have turned it over to you."

"It's a lot of money for someone to say they don't want. I mean, I understand it, but I don't like it." He nodded, then shook his head at her. "You think I should take it?"

"Yes...yes, ma'am, I do. You can do a powerful lot of good with that much money. More'n them people up there in them offices have ever done for any of us vets, or the homeless for that matter. That new shelter you're putting in? You can sure fill it with a lot of nice things for us old men and women to use. Beds with nice mattresses on them. Sheets that don't have no holes in them. Yes, ma'am, you sure can make a big difference in a lot of sad, lonely lives with that much cash." He nodded to the envelope. "Cash money to give out when there ain't no money for meds. A couple of bucks to tide one over in the event that the check is late. Doctors ain't cheap. You can help a person out to get to one that they might not have afforded before."

She fingered the money, and he knew that she was thinking of whatever that boy had told her...broke her heart, whatever it had been. Craig knew that he'd be a sorry man if Andi's husband was there now, but then again, maybe not. That Mac, he was a good man, just like his daddy.

"He said to not name it for his mother. He told me that she no more deserved that than she did to have him and Lizzy as her children. He'd come to take it back if I did that." Craig had known Martha and the person that she was. Most hadn't, or if they did, they never said anything to her. She was a mean old cuss, and had been as a kid too. "You think that she'd be rolling over in her grave, knowing that the money she hoarded for years is going to help a lot of people out that she wouldn't before? If for no other reason than that, I'm thinking of using the money as you said — to help people out when they need it the most."

"I'm thinking that old Martha got just what she deserved and if that boy was my son, I'd be right proud to call him my own." Craig pointed to the money again. "He could have done left that money in the house when they tore it down. Not caring a fig for whoever might have dug them a basement someday and found it. But he thought of you, and what you might do with it. I heard him saying to you that he'd been checking you out. He knew just what he was doing in coming here and leaving that to you. Formed a trust in you that many don't get told to them."

"There might be more, he told me." Craig tried to think how on earth that woman had hidden away so much money, but said nothing to Andi. She was hurting enough right now. "He's taking some of it home to his sister. He's sure that I'll be getting that too. Neither of them wanted anything to do with their mother after they left here. He said that Lizzy has been going to see a shrink since she was a little girl, and that while it helped them both, neither of them have had children, nor have they dated all that much. I can't imagine doing something so…beyond cruel to your own son and daughter. Can you?"

"No, I rightly can't. But then, I was raised in a loving home, with my parents scraping every penny together to make our lives better. But I knew Drew's daddy, the one that gave them two a name, that is. A good man he was." Andi looked at him then, her mind leaving the money and it's meaning behind for a minute. "Married old Martha when she was big with somebody else's babe…that little girl, it turned out. Little Drew, he was already borned by then; his daddy had died before he'd been brought in this here world, and Martha had…well, she wasn't a nice person, so we all wondered at how somebody got to…you know. But Barker wanted her to have a good name, he told me, but there was no helping her with her disposition, I guess. Martha was born a nasty woman, and she died as one. Old Barker, he passed some years back, a happy man for leaving her behind."

"Did he have another family? Maybe they'd want this money." He told her that he'd become something of an honorary uncle for children at the hospital where he lived, giving them small gifts and trinkets when he visited. "So he really was a good man. Maybe we could name the building for him."

"Nah, he'd not like that anymore than the kids wanted that money. You name it for what it is, girl: a shelter." She looked at the money, then at him again. "You thinking that you can't take it still? I suppose you can just put it in your house, let the dust fall over it again for another fifty or so years. Or you can hoard it; seems money tainted with her touch might as well go on not being used."

"You're very slick, aren't you, Mr. Craig?" He asked her what she meant, quite proud, actually, that she'd seen through him. "Comparing me to Martha in this. I'm not going to let it get dusty again. I'm going to use if for good, not evil. But you owe me."

"Me? I didn't do a damned thing that you'd think I owe you." Then she told him what it was going to be. "Oh. I can see you wanting me to run the shelter. But I'm an old man…won't be around for that much longer, you know. I'll do what I can, but you should maybe find you a younger man, one that'll be around for another few years after I been able to teach him all that I know." He laughed with her, and he knew that whatever demons had been in her head and heart were gone. For now, anyways. Craig loved this woman like she was his own child.

She got up then, putting the heavy envelope in her apron pocket. Then she leaned over him, taking off his ball cap, and kissed him right on the head. Damned if he didn't feel it right to his toes when she did that. Looking up at her, Craig asked her why she'd done a fool thing like that.

"Because, Mr. Craig, I love you." And with that she moved away, and he sat there dumbfounded for ten minutes. When he stood up, Craig felt like he'd been given a new lease on life. Damned if it didn't feel right good having someone kissing him on the head for being an old man.

CHAPTER 14

"I'd like for you to think about this for a few days. A week at the very least before you feel you have to give me an answer." Aedan nodded, his heart feeling like someone had put electrodes to it. "Aedan? You can tell me no...you know that, don't you?"

"I doubt very much that you'd let me." The president, Harold he'd been asked to call him, only nodded and leaned back in his chair. Here he was, in the personal home of one of the most powerful men in the world, and they were both having a glass of wine and eating pizza like he was one of his old buddies from college. "Why me, if you don't mind me asking? I mean, there are a great many people out there that can do a better job simply because they have more experience."

"True. There are. But none of them have the heart that you do." The cigar, not lit but still chewed upon, hung from the other man's mouth as he continued. "Do you have any idea what sort of work you can do as the governor of your own state? What sort of jobs you can create just by your name alone?"

"There are several businesses that I can name that would come there, with the right incentive." Harold smiled at him but said nothing. "You're banking on my name then, not me."

"No. Some of it, but not all. You're a good man, raised by good people, and it does help that your last name is Harrison. And of course that your sister-in-law is none other than Storm Browning. But that's not all of it." Aedan started to ask him what else when he stood up and moved to the table on the other side of the room. When he returned with a thick file with his name on it, Aedan just held it. "You should see the things that we know about you."

Instead of opening it, like his fingers burned to do, he tossed it on the desk. "I know what sort of man I am. I worked hard to get me there. Of course my mother would tell you it was all her doing, and my dad would tell you that I took after him. Which, by the way, are both true."

"See? A humble man even in the face of all this." Aedan leaned back too, thinking that he'd only come here today to get some paperwork for Storm. She'd set him up, he just knew it. He asked him about it. "Yes. Stormy knows what I'm about. In fact, she told me you'd turn me down flat, something about making your own way by moving up slowly through the ranks."

"And she would be correct." Aedan sat there, thinking of all the things he'd planned out for his life. One step at a time, taking his time learning the job before moving on. "I was going to run for governor first, and then maybe taking a second term before branching out for the next level of running for your job before I found me a mate and settled down."

"You can have it. And to be honest with you, Aedan, I have hopes of you sitting right here one day soon. But taking on the governorship now is a step in the right direction." Aedan told him he was joking. "I'm not. A

Harrison here, in the White House? Perfect. I'll vote for you."

"I'm not ready for that." Harold nodded and continued to chew on his cigar. "I have a feeling that I'm going to be taking the governorship job and doing more work for you in the meantime."

"Yes." Harold laughed as he turned and looked at him. "When I tell your mother, and I will if you don't, what do you think she's going to do?"

"Figure out a way to get in here and try to redecorate your offices. Then see about finding me a mate so I can have her grandchild in the White House. There has already been a wedding here. A grandbaby would make her day. Hell, her life." Harold laughed. "I'm not going to find a mate until I have my own life settled. I have things I want to do, and having a wife to care for is not part of that plan. Not yet."

"You think a wife is a burden to you?" He told him no, but she would require him to change his plans. "Why? I mean, Storm didn't require your brother to do any such thing."

"No, she didn't *require* it, but he's different. Sappy, if you want to know the truth. I don't want to appear to be led around by my balls, thanks." Harold laughed. "I love women. All of them. And would love to someday, later down the line, meet my own true love. But way down the line, and not until I have done what I want done. I don't want to think about every move because there is someone else involved in my life."

"So you think having a mate would somehow ruin your chances of becoming the president of the free world." Aedan nodded. "Not very PC of you, young man. When you're sitting here, as a single man, every woman in the world is going to want to have a hunk of you."

"Fine. To a point. But you know as well as I do that there is only one person for me, and when she comes along, it'll have to be after I'm done sitting there." Aedan knew he sounded like an ass, and if his mother or father heard him, he'd be in deep shit. But a mate or wife changed a man. Both his brothers were proof of that.

"You give it some thought and get back to me. I'll be here for the next four years or so, and you know how to contact me too if you have any questions." He stood up, thinking he was being dismissed. "Come on down to my real offices. I want you to get a feel for the room. You'll get your own chair, of course, but it'll be yours soon enough."

After the meeting of sorts was over, Aedan made his way back to Riordan's home they had purchased here in DC. It was way bigger than his at home...servants out the ass, as well as a pool that was not only heated but covered as well. Going there now, he dove into the water and swam several laps before he let himself think about what he'd just talked about.

President. President Aedan Harrison. Smiling, he loved the sound of that. Not right now. He wasn't stupid and knew that he had a great deal to learn about the job before he even began to say the words aloud, but damn, did he want to do it.

Aedan had always had big plans. Even as a child he'd worked hard for something if he wanted it, and kept it nice in the event that one day he'd get bored or tired of it and wish to sell it. He knew even at ten that money made the world work, and he'd made sure that he learned how to care for that as well. He was, if he did say so himself, good at figuring out his own worth and how to make it more. He supposed all of them had been, but he'd worked harder.

He was rich. Not like Stormy was, who was worth billions, but he had close to his first billon now. And by the time he was ready to take the office, he wanted there to be no questions of his taking money from others to do things for them. Aedan wanted to be a self-made man, and he was going to do it.

As he made his way up to the room he was using, he wondered why Harold had seemed fixated on a mate. Aedan didn't have a problem with having one, was in fact looking forward to having one at his side. But he also knew that they could make or break a man that had big plans, and he was, for even as young as he was, sort of set in his ways. A mate, at this time in his life, would not be welcome at all.

But would he run for governor? Yes. He would. It was what he wanted, maybe not in the order he had wanted, but it was the stepping stone for what he had worked out. Just a little earlier than he'd wanted. Rolling to his back, he wanted to call his mom and tell her and Dad, but knew that they'd keep him up all night with questions, and he wanted to just savor the thought of it for a little while on his own.

He didn't have the seat yet either, his mind told him. It was just an open slot that he could run for. Yes, that was true. There were no guarantees that he'd even win the race, and he'd have to start all over again if he didn't.

Closing his eyes, willing his body to shut down, he smiled one more time and thought of himself as governor. He'd be able to do so many things with that position. And with the help of his family, he knew that he'd be good at it too.

~~~

"No." Nikki hated that word almost as she did the stupid phrase "these ones." Christ, what the fuck were they teaching kids in school these days? "You hear me, bitch. I said I ain't gonna flip for you."

"I didn't ask you to flip, dumbass. All I asked you to do was to tell me who was selling you the drugs in the first place. I want to make him a better deal." The man at her feet, handcuffed to the fence behind him, snorted at her. "You don't think I can deal, Rojas? I can, you know. And I play a mean game of pool too."

He eyed her. "What the Sam biscuits does pool have to do with this shit? Are you trying to get me killed here?" She didn't even bother answering him. "Ah, that's cold. Real cold. After I done went and let you capture me and shit."

"Yes, you were very generous by letting me run you down for five city blocks before you ran into a parked car, falling on your ass. Very helpful, that was. What do you do for an encore?" He only stared at her. "Never mind. I want their name, Rojas. When you give it to me, I'll let you call your momma and let her know you won't be home for dinner."

"You know my momma ain't home. You jacked her up three weeks ago. And now you're giving me the same shit. Don't you have better things to do?" Nikki pretended to think about it. "You are one cold bitch. Anyone ever tell you that?"

"Yes. My ex-husband. He was just like you. A little shit that should have known better than to fuck with me." Looking for her partner, she wasn't surprised to see him walking toward her like he'd run a marathon and come out at the end of the race. The man had to be fifty pounds overweight, and a heart attack away from leaving this job on a permanent basis. He walked up to the car that Rojas had run into and leaned heavily against it, heaving and breathing hard.

"You should have waited on me. You know I could have been helpful in getting him down." Nikki said nothing. "My captain said to tell you that you're done with this one until he talks to you."

"Why?" He only shrugged. "Well, it matters little. I don't work for your captain. I have my own."

The cruiser pulled up beside them a few minutes later. Nikki was undercover and had been for about six months now. But she knew as well as the cops around her that her cover was blown and she really was done. As she made her way to her own car, sixteen blocks away, she thought of the nice long vacation she was going to take as soon as she was debriefed. Her cell phone ringing made her smile.

"Hello, Grandda. How's it hanging?" He laughed at her and she smiled bigger. "They're pulling me here. I'll be home in a few hours. Do you wanna have some pizza and a few beers?"

"I'd rather have a thick steak with all the trimmings, if you don't mind." Sounded good to her. "Good. You can swing by here, pick this old man up, and we'll go out in style."

The car paused as it came around the corner toward her. She answered her grandda and told him that she'd be there. When he asked her what was wrong, she wasn't going to lie to him. He'd been a cop too. Then an undercover agent with the Feds.

"There's a black two-door watching me." She gave him the plate number. "Can't see how many are in it. Tinted and up."

"Take a turn when you can." She went into the first store that was open. "Where are you? The place you went in?"

"Mason's Bakery." She looked out the window as she stood in line at the counter. When it was her turn, she ordered sourdough and two Danish. "I can't stay here. If there is a problem, I can't bring it down on them."

"Right. When you leave there, make a left onto James Street. There is a lot of traffic there and you might be able to lose them in the stream." She paid for her bread and headed out of the door. The car was gone and she told him that, but neither of them thought it was done. "James Street, Nikki. Go there."

"I'm headed that way now." As soon as she turned onto James, she realized it was over. "Grandda. I love you. They're here."

"Mother fuck balls." Even in her fear she smiled as she lowered her phone, but didn't close the connection. There were two cars waiting for her, ten men, all armed with various guns and assault rifles. The man she'd been chasing for six months was leaning unarmed against the same black car that had been at the corner.

"You looking for me?" Nikki said nothing as the man moved toward her. "I hear tell it that you've been trying to make some sort of deal with me. Like I want to deal with a fucking cop like you."

"I'm not a cop." He snorted at her, something that she knew if she lived, she was never going to do again. "I'm an undercover cop. Special like, to get scum like you off the streets. You willing to turn yourself in, I'm sure I can accommodate you and your friends."

"You trying to be funny?" She told him she was considered very funny by most. "Well, I ain't most. I don't think you're funny at all."

"Good to know. You have no sense of humor. What do you plan to do, Otis, kill an undercover cop while she's on duty?" He was handed a gun and Nikki wanted to turn and run. But she knew, as he more than likely did, she had nowhere to go. "Not very sporting of you to gun me down with all these men just watching us."

"They're going to have their piece of you too." Nodding, she looked around at the other men. Any one of them was more than likely on a list somewhere. Murder more than likely being at the top of the list. "You're dead, cop. You just ain't fell to the ground yet."

Nodding, she sent a small prayer of thanks that her grandda would be taken care of. He had help if he needed it, and if she was killed now, he'd have her pension as well as her insurance. When Otis told her to go to her knees, she did so. There was no hope to survive this now. But as she lowered herself to the sidewalk, she snapped as many pictures as she could, hoping that someone would find them.

The first shot took her breath away as it entered her chest. The next one hit her in the thigh, and she knew that it was going to be a long time coming, her death. But when she fell back, her entire body being slammed by bullets, she heard her grandda screaming in the phone that they were coming. She had no idea why he thought they weren't already there.

Before You Go...

HELP AN AUTHOR
write a review
THANK YOU!

Share your voice and help guide other readers to these wonderful books. Even if it's only a line or two your reviews help readers discover the author's books so they can continue creating stories that you'll love. Login to your favorite retailer and leave a review. Thank you.

AWARD WINNING, BESTSELLING AUTHOR

Kathi Barton, author of the bestselling series Force of Nature, lives in Nashport, Ohio with her husband Paul. In addition to writing full time Kathi likes to spend time with her eight grandkids, three children and three children-in-laws. She writes to relax and have fun.

Her muse, a cross between Jimmy Stewart and Hugh Jackman brings them to life for her readers in a way that has them coming back time and again for more. Her favorite genre is paranormal romance with a great deal of spice. You can visit Kathi on line and drop her an email if you'd like. She loves hearing from her fans. aaronskiss@gmail.com.

Follow Kathi on her blog:
http://kathisbartonauthor.blogspot.com/

www.ingramcontent.com/pod-product-compliance
Lightning Source LLC
Chambersburg PA
CBHW032128170626
46808CB00006B/2151